The Case of the Pink Macaw

A Tale of Sexton Blake,

Tinker and the Black Eagle.

From The Sexton Blake Library,
Series 1, No. 371. 31 March, 1925.

by G. H. Teed

Stillwoods Edition 2019.

Stillwoods.Blogspot.Ca

Catalogue Information:
Title: The Case of the Pink Macaw
Author: G. H. Teed (1886-1938)
First Published: Sexton Blake Library, Series 1, No. 371. 31 March, 1925.
Original cover illustrated by Arthur Jones and adapted.
This Edition: Stillwoods, 2019
ISBN Canada: 978-1-988304-75-5
Blog: Stillwoods.Blogspot.Ca
Author's Blog: http://ghteed.blogspot.com/
Storefront: http://www.lulu.com/spotlight/lulubook22

Keywords: Sexton Blake, The Black Eagle, British detective fiction

Synopsis:
The Black Eagle swears vengeance on the trader, Bully Blood as he rescues a young lad and his 'Pink Macaw' from the captain's brutality.

Years later, that Captain has become Barnfield Gore; and at a private gambling session, he is poisoned and attacked by a Pink Macaw, even as Sexton Blake watches!

More intrigue enters when Detective-Inspector Thomas seeks out Blake to help him with yet another gruesome murder.

The investigation of these events is dramatic and results in some ferocious battles for Blake and Tinker!

"Four New Volumes of the Sexton Blake Library are issued on the first Friday of every month. Please give your Newsagent a Standing Order for them."

MOSTLY he was known as Captain Blood wherever he sailed, and that meant all over the seven seas which are known and charted, and into seven hundred bays and lagoons and jungle-lined creeks and bays which are not charted, except in the minds of men like Captain Blood, who have their own reasons for going there.

That wasn't his real name, any more than was the "Blood Ship" the real name of the dirty old schooner he sailed; but if you spoke of either among seafaring men in any part of the world, there wasn't one but knew whom and what ship you meant.

On the schooner's manifests and in her papers he was, of course, called something else, and in formal talk agents and consignors and consignees called him thus.

There were men, too, who had sailed under him who named him worse; but generally, on the high seas among other craft, and ashore in the saloons and dives and "crimps" lodging-houses, it was "Captain Blood" or "Bully Blood," and the "Blood Ship."

That wasn't the first time or the only time that a man had earned that name for himself, and a capper for his ship, but there could have been few occasions when the designation was more merited.

There were plenty of men still afloat who had known him, actually or by rumour, back when he was a bucko mate sailing out of 'Frisco in a hell ship, which never could have got a crew if it hadn't been for the crimps. But no one seemed to know just how or when he had got a hooker of his own. There seemed in the talk about him a patch, so to say, during which time he had disappeared as a bucko mate and had reappeared as skipper of his own ship.

Down through the South Seas one heard bits of rumour here and there— gossip dropped along the bar where seafaring men foregather—and, pieced together, those patches might be fashioned into a queer tale.

For instance, there was a time when, it was said, the sometime bucko mate had given up the sea and had settled on one of the outer and little known islands of the Marquesas. Some kanakas probably spread that, and, from the same source or a casual schooner, it is likely that the story gained ground that he had hitched up with a trader there, had married the trader's daughter—a lithe and exotic half-caste, scarce into her teens—and had taken over control of the trade and sweating the copra from the natives.

Then there seems to have been another hiatus, for it was said that a trading schooner had visited the island and found the trading shack and godown destroyed, with plenty of marks to show that they had been gutted by fire. The natives scattered, and either too ignorant of what had happened or too scared to tell a coherent tale, and no signs of the trader or his daughter and her husband.

It was a bit of the story that no man was ever destined to pick up, but, some months later, the whilom bucko mate sailed into Sydney harbour as skipper of his own schooner. And from that period begins the history of Captain Blood.

In those days he was a big, upstanding man of under thirty with the quick step of the man whose leg muscles are beautifully sprung, and the reposeful arms of the natural fighter. He had grown a tangled black beard that twisted to a point, and leant added menace to the deep-set sinister cold eyes that had cowed many a husky in the past.

As a bucko mate he had not been disinclined to mix to some extent with men of his own calling and rank, but as skipper he kept aloof from his fellowmen, his sole intercourse being almost entirely confined to those with whom he had business. And he never seemed to find it difficult to pick up a cargo, for, whatever else he was, Blood was a finished and daring seaman, and chalked up quick passage after quick passage in a way that made even the iron tanks look slow at times.

It was whispered that he carried queer cargoes in some parts of the seven seas, and there may have been something in the gossip, for the dingy old schooner had a habit of bobbing up in the most unexpected places, in little-known bays, and off muddy rivers of barren stretches of the China Coast, under the lea of an island fragment in the southern Phillipines, where the Moros were in revolt, perhaps off the coast of a South American Republic where a revolution was in progress; or even in the well-patrolled waters off the Atlantic or Pacific coast of America, where there was much money to be had for running in a cargo of spirits, or a bunch of unauthorised immigrants,

It is said that there are few places left to-day where the boarding-house of the old-time crimp flourishes, or where a lone sailorman is in danger of being shanghaied, but those who tell one that either don't know the truth, or they speak with a tongue in cheek. There are plenty of ships like Blood's which would never sail with a full complement if it were not for the assistance of the crimps.

That was Captain Blood, and that was his ship at the time he was lying off a mangrove-lined shore, on a certain part of the coast of South America with the old schooner dipping and rolling under the gentle swell of the lower Caribbean, while the crew, or some of it, lay lolling about the deck sweltering under the blaze of the tropic sun.

On the poop the mate, a hard-bitten Yankee from Maine walked back and forth, back and forth, his lean jaws champing in a regular motion as he ground a quid of black twist between his yellow teeth, and his eyes ever and anon seeking the flat line of the shore half a mile or so distant.

Captain Blood was below as was the second mate, and perhaps it was for this reason that those of the crew who were on deck took their case, for, though he was a hard driver, the mate was no bucko, and when not under the glare of the cold black eyes and the soft mocking whisper of the captain's voice, was inclined to treat his watch like human beings.

The ship had cast anchor off the coast early that morning after a good run down from a certain American port where she had taken on a cargo of "agricultural implements" and "sewing machines."

It might seem odd that there could be much of a market for such goods in a country which was at the time in the throes of a revolution; but, when the chance offered, Captain Blood had not wasted much time in a study of the economic situation of his coast of destination, but, after some argument about the rate of freight, had clinched the deal.

And it might also have appeared odd that such a cargo should be lying offshore waiting for the night to come when it would be quietly loaded into small boats and landed at a deserted part of the coast; but that again was part of the contract, and Captain Blood was the sort of man who took a pride in carrying out to the letter agreement with consignors and consignees. So the ship with all hands panted under the sun of early afternoon waiting for the purple curtain of night to descend.

It was during the course of his pacing on the poop that the mate suddenly came to a pause, and screwed up his eyes as he peered across the water at a small speck which seemed just then to detach itself from the shore. He watched it for some time until it drew farther and farther away from the shore and resolved itself into a small boat which seemed to be heading in the direction of the ship.

As the minutes passed, it was obvious that it was making for the schooner, and, leaning his arms on the rail, the mate watched it while he gradually made out that there seemed to be three persons in it, one at the oars, one seated in the stern and one in the bow. Some of the crew had also spotted the little craft and dragged themselves to the rail also to watch.

Those in the boat did not seem to pay much attention to the schooner or its human complement until the oarsman swung round sideways so that the rowboat would lie side on and then he lay resting on his oars and waited.

The mate could now make out that the two passengers were undoubtedly sailormen, one being a dark-visaged person whose face and form called for a second look, and the other, a youngster with a round red face and a thick shock of flaming red hair. On the latter's shoulder was perched a giant macaw, one of the biggest specimens of the bird which the mate had ever seen, and of a blush pink of body and crest, and indigo of wing and tail which were new to him.

The pink looked odd in contrast to the flaming red of the young fellow's hair, and the big powerful curved beak of the superparrot seemed thick enough and sharp enough to gouge the youth's throat clean open in a single stroke if the macaw had felt in a murderous mood.

But its owner seemed on the best of terms with his pet, for while the keen-faced man in the stern gazed in silence for a few minutes at the mate, he stroked and ruffled the bird's crest causing it to lurch about on his shoulder in an ecstacy of enjoyment. And then the man in the stern spoke.

"Are you the captain?" he asked, in a tone that was deep and sharp and carried across the intervening stretch of water without effort.

The mate spat into the water and shook his head.

"The old man is below," he answered, in a strong nasal twang. "What do you want?"

"To sign on both of us. Are you shorthanded?"

The mate grinned, and some of the crew began to whisper among themselves at this, but then grew suddenly silent as the mate swung his head and glared at them. Then he made answer:

"That depends. We are not crowded, and if you two know your job we might find room for you. How comes it you are looking for a berth off the coast like this?"

"We came up the coast in a native craft," answered the man in the small boat almost rudely. "The whole country is upside down with a revolution. We want to get north—to America or Europe—it doesn't matter. We are both able-bodied seamen, and not afraid of work."

"Well, if you like to come aboard and wait I'll speak to the captain when he comes on deck. I don't say he will or he won't. You'll have to take your chance." But when the other asked if they should keep the small boat waiting, the mate said they might as well let it return to the shore. So the man in the stern spoke a word to the oarsman, and a few moments later he and his companion came over the side.

They each had a bundle, and one of the crew good-naturedly volunteered to show them a place in the fo'c'sle where they could pitch their dunnage, for there wasn't a man there but knew the pair would be signed on quick enough. And there were plenty to whisper a warning to the newcomers of the sort of ship she was, and the sort of captain who commanded her, but to this the pair only smiled and said they would take a chance on any blankety skipper on the seven seas.

But none of the crew knew that of all the living creatures on the earth, Captain Blood had a fierce and undying hatred of the sort of bird which the round-faced youth had brought aboard. Somewhere in that murky past of his Bully Blood had found reason for this feeling, and if the pair of newcomers had guessed for a single moment that the very bird which the youngster carried was none other than the one which was the cause of this hatred, they would have been well advised to get away then and there.

But they did not know this, nor did they know Captain Blood, for the younger man had not been afloat long enough, and the other had for some years been in a place where he learnt little or nothing of what went on in the great world.

So they stood about the deck with the others while the westering sun dropped lower and lower, and the crew talked idly of the toil which the night would bring. And then, all of a sudden, every man-jack seemed to feel a "something" that brought him to his feet, and sent him to this spot or that on a pretence of performing some trifling bit of work, while, under lowered lids, nervous eyes were bent in the direction of the poop.

The two newcomers found themselves standing alone, and then they, too, turned to gaze aft, and as they did so they saw the dark, menacing countenance of Captain Blood as he emerged from the companionway and swung slowly to sweep the ship with his gaze.

They saw him, too, as his eyes lit on them, and then came to rest on the great macaw, which was exhibiting signs of agitation as it gripped and ungripped its claws in the shoulders of the young fellow who bore it, causing him to wince with the pain.

And then there seemed to follow a queer silence, which was finally broken by the whispering voice of Captain Blood as he addressed his mate.

"Mister," he said, "mister, where did you pick up this scum, and who brought that foul bird aboard my ship?"

And men who knew Captain Blood knew what that tone meant.

So the reader gets an idea of the nature of the original publication some 95 years ago! At scale and existing intensity; scanner at 400dpi.

this feeling, and if the pair of newcomers had guessed for a single moment that the very bird which the youngster carried was none other than the one which was the cause of this hatred, they would have been well advised to get away then and there.

But they did not know this, nor did they know Captain Blood, for the younger man had not been afloat long enough, and the other had for some years been in a place where he learnt little or nothing of what went on in the great world.

So they stood about the deck with the others while the westering sun dropped lower and lower, and the crew talked idly of the toil which the night would bring. And then, all of a sudden, every man-jack seemed to feel a "something" that brought him to his feet, and sent him to this spot or that on a pretence of performing some trifling bit of work, while, under lowered lids, nervous eyes were bent in the direction of the poop.

The two newcomers found themselves standing alone, and then they, too, turned to gaze aft, and as they did so they saw the dark, menacing countenance of Captain Blood as he emerged from the companion-way and swung slowly to sweep the ship with his gaze.

They saw him, too, as his eyes lit on them, and then came to rest on the great macaw, which was exhibiting signs of agitation as it gripped and ungripped its claws in the shoulders of the young fellow who bore it, causing him to wince with the pain.

And then there seemed to follow a queer silence, which was finally broken by the whispering voice of Captain Blood as he addressed his mate.

"Mister," he said, "mister, where did you pick up this scum, and who brought that foul bird aboard my ship?"

And men who knew Captain Blood knew what that tone meant.

———

II

The Man from Devil's Island.

BRIEFLY, the Yankee mate explained how the two men had come aboard while the captain was asleep below, and all the time Blood stood looking at the pink macaw. And the pink macaw sat clinging to the young fellow's shoulder staring back unblinkingly at Blood.

It was a strange little tableau that, on the deck of the old hooker, with the swell of the Caribbean rocking the schooner with great swings from side to side, and the low shore of the Spanish Main making their horizon to the south.

Farm machinery and sewing-machines! That was the cargo the ship's manifest showed; but not a man-jack aboard but knew the cases of farm machinery contained machine guns and rifles, and the cases of sewing-machines nothing else but closely packed boxes of ammunition. For Captain Blood was, for the time being, engaged in the profitable occupation of gun-running, and ashore, behind the line of mangroves, men lay even then in waiting until the curtain of night should drop down as a cover to the work of unloading.

But Captain Bully Blood was not thinking then of his cargo. Nor was he paying but a vagrant attention to what the mate was saying. Instead, his mind had travelled many thousands of leagues away. Just then he was picturing a certain lagoon in the South Pacific where, two years before, he had seen just another pink macaw as that one which stared at him now.

Another one? Or was it the same? That was what Blood was asking himself, and, as an incident of that other day was recalled to his mind, he lifted one heavy hand and touched his neck under the left ear. His black beard grew thick just there; but if one had been standing close one might have seen, as he parted the hair, a long, white, irregular mark—an old scar which might have been done by some jagged instrument, or even the heavy curved beak of a bird such as a macaw.

And then, suddenly, in the stillness which reigned as the mate finished speaking, the macaw began heaving itself up and down, and, opening its vicious beak, gave vent to a shrill, mocking scream. It was devilish, that pagan sound in the stillness of the afternoon, and the chuckle which followed the scream was even more satanic.

On Bully Blood it seemed to act like a blow in the face. Above the black beard his face went suddenly livid, and his eyes narrowed as the pupils seemed to reveal some inward flame. But not until the macaw had again become still did he make a move. Then he said, without turning his head:

"Mister, send below for my fowling-piece.

7

II   The Man from Devil's Island.

BRIEFLY, the Yankee mate explained how the two men had come aboard while the captain was asleep below, and all the time Blood stood looking at the pink macaw. And the pink macaw sat clinging to the young fellow's shoulder staring back unthinkingly at Blood.

It was a strange little tableau that, on the deck of the old hooker, with the swell of the Caribbean rocking the schooner with great swings from side to side, and the low shore of the Spanish Main making their horizon to the south.

Farm machinery and sewing-machines! That was the cargo the ship's manifest showed; but not a man-jack aboard but knew the cases of farm machinery contained machine guns and rifles, and the cases of sewing-machines nothing else but closely packed boxes of ammunition. For Captain Blood was, for the time being, engaged in the profitable occupation of gun-running, and ashore, behind the line of mangroves, men lay even then in waiting until the curtain of night should drop down as a cover to the work of unloading.

But Captain Bully Blood was not thinking then of his cargo. Nor was he paying but a vagrant attention to what the mate was saying. Instead, his mind had travelled many thousands of leagues away. Just then he was picturing a certain lagoon in the South Pacific where, two years before, he had seen just another pink macaw as that one which stared at him now.

Another one? Or was it the same? That was what Blood was asking himself, and, as an incident of that other day was recalled to his mind, he lifted one heavy hand and touched his neck under the left ear. His black beard grew thick just there; but if one had been standing close one might have seen, as he parted the hair, a long, white, irregular mark—an old scar which might have been done by some jagged instrument, or even the heavy curved beak of a bird such as a macaw.

And then, suddenly, in the stillness which reigned as the mate finished speaking, the macaw began heaving itself up and down, and, opening its vicious beak, gave vent to a shrill, mocking scream. It was devilish, that pagan sound in the stillness of the afternoon, and the chuckle which followed the scream was even more satanic.

On Bully Blood it seemed to act like a blow in the face. Above the black beard his face went suddenly livid, and his eyes narrowed as the pupils seemed to reveal some inward flame. But not until the macaw had again become still did he make a move. Then he said, without turning his head:

"Mister, send below for my fowling-piece. I'll have no blanked screaming bird aboard my ship."

The Yankee mate hesitated, then he walked to the companionway and shouted down to the cabin-boy, giving that youth the captain's message. In the meantime, Blood beckoned to the two strangers, who had been too far away to hear his command to the mate, and who now walked aft towards where he stood.

As they paused in front of him, he gazed down from his elevated position on the poop and examined them critically. He was thus engaged when the cabin-boy put in an appearance bearing a double-barrelled shotgun. It was a modern weapon, but it was a habit of Blood's to refer to it by the old-fashioned term of "fowling-piece."

The cabin-boy stood nervously behind the captain while the latter still continued to gaze down at the pair who awaited his verdict. The taller of the two had been completely impassive since setting foot on the deck. He had given back stare for stare, but not by the flicker of an eyelash did he betray what his opinion might be of Captain Blood.

As for the more impetuous young fellow beside him, his Celtic blood had arisen at the first words the captain had uttered, and now, as he saw the cabin-boy holding the shotgun, he was looking puzzled. Some instinct told him that Blood meant mischief towards his bird.

As for the macaw, it was still gazing in the same canny, unblinking way at Blood, but what it might be thinking no man might know. The Yankee mate, who had sailed many a voyage with Blood, knew the signs only too well, and he was now standing back against the rail waiting to see what would happen.

And then, all of a sudden, Blood's black beard parted as he smiled, showing teeth startlingly white in contrast.

"So you want to sail in this ship, do you?" he said, in the same toneless whisper. "Well, we have room for you, my men. But you can't bring that blanked screaming bird with you, and, just to make sure, I am going to blow it to pieces now."

"You are not going to shoot my macaw," cried the youth, suddenly stiffening. "Where I go, my bird goes. If you don't want it here I'll go back to the shore."

"Talk back to me, you scum, and I'll pick your flesh off in pieces," whispered Blood, still showing his teeth. "You come aboard my ship without leave. You can swim if you want to take a chance with the sharks. But that bird goes to glory now." Then, without turning his head, he went on, speaking to the mate: "Mister, have this scum held while I kill that bird."

The mate, to do him justice, had no taste for the job; but he knew Bully Blood, and he knew what would happen to him if he showed resistance. So he barked out an order, and at the command a dozen men sprang forward.

There wasn't a man aboard but didn't hate Bully Blood with every ounce of his heart and soul, but, on the other hand, every man's prospects were bound up with those of Blood, and every man held him in deadly fear. So there was no hesitation when the mate barked out the order.

The red-headed boy resisted and struggled futilely while half a dozen husky sailormen bore him to the deck, while the macaw flew round and round screaming out curses in a frenzy of rage. As for the other man, he had uttered a few quick words to the boy, warning him of the futility of resistance; then he stood quietly, allowing himself to be seized and held.

It was just the difference in attitude of the hot-headed youth who still had to learn what the world held, and that of the seasoned man who knew how to bide his time when the odds were overwhelming.

When the pair stood quietly in the grip of their captors, Captain Blood spoke again, while his narrowed eyes watched the course of the macaw which was still wheeling about, spitting out its rage in screams and harsh, throaty threats.

"Get me that bird, someone," he said. "You—you scum," he went on, referring to the red-headed youth, "call that blanked fury down, and keep it quiet."

"I'll do nothing," raged the boy. "If you harm that bird I'll kill you, as sure as I live. If you think you or any of your crew can catch him, then try it. And you can't shoot well enough to hit him while he is on the wing."

And then, as if it understood what the boy said, the macaw, with a final screech of jeering rage, rose and rose clear to the cross-trees, where it settled and shook its ruffled plumage. Bully Blood reached behind him and took the shotgun from the cabin boy. He glanced at the breach to see if the loading was in order, then, with an extraordinarily quick motion, he jerked the gun to his shoulder and both barrels crashed out.

But if Bully Blood was quick, the pink macaw was quicker, for, although both charges of lead scattered about the crosstrees where the macaw had been clinging, the bird was no longer there, and in screaming flight reached the mainmast cross-trees, where it clung, heaving up and down and spitting out jeers at Blood. It was almost human the way the bird hurled defiance at him.

The red-headed youth laughed and mocked also at Blood. "Try again," he cried. "You can shoot away every cartridge you have, and you won't hit him."

Blood's face was even more livid than before, if that were possible. He did not reply then to the taunt, but something seemed to tell him that the boy was right, and that if he persisted in his present course he would only succeed in making an exhibition of himself in front of the crew.

But Bully Blood had dealt with every phase of shipboard situations in his time, and he reckoned he knew a trick or two that would soon turn the boy's mockery into something very different.

It was an evil chance of Fate that at that moment the second mate, roused probably by the sound of the gun, came on deck to see what was going on. He was a very different type from the Yankee mate, and was hand-in-glove with every bit of devilry Bully Blood had pulled off for years past.

He was far more in Blood's confidence than the mate, and would have filled the first's place had it not been that he was a drunkard, and Bully Blood was not the man to give the chief control of his ship to any man who might be lying drunk in his berth when a typhoon might be kicking them across the Yellow Sea, or the sudden break of the monsoon might sweep down upon them in the Indian Ocean.

But in all other matters the second was his chief lieutenant. And now, as he took in the situation and saw the pink macaw high up on the mainmast, cross-trees, a curious expression came over his face, and he turned and looked at Blood. "Sink me, captain," he began, but Blood cut him short.

"Mister Creed," he said, "do you recall how we handled the tribal chief at Matonga?"

"Yes, sir," answered the second, with a grin.

"Then, Mister Creed, take me this redheaded scum and do the same with him. Look sharp, mister. It will be dark soon, and we have work to do."

The mate had not been with Blood on the occasion to which he had referred, but the second knew only too well what he meant; and there were a few of the crew, too, who had been at Matonga, in the Solomons, when the chief of the tribe there had been man-handled after Blood had recruited every able-bodied man in the tribe for the plantations. And to some of these old hands the second mate made a sign.

The tall, dark, stern-faced man who stood beside the boy watched in silence as several men began running in different directions, getting together ropes and a big pulley block. Then two of them went up the ratlines to the foremast cross-trees, and there one of them hitched the block over one shoulder and continued on up the topmast rigging until he reached the top.

He clung there, bending on the block, and all eyes were on him as he swung back and forth in a great arc as the ship rolled in the swell, but, even when he saw him work the end of a rope through the block and ease the end down to his companion at the cross-trees, the elder of the two prisoners did not guess what was up.

But then, as the boy was dragged across the deck and hauled up towards the crosstrees, he suddenly grasped what devilry was afoot. For the first time he began to struggle, but soon saw that he hadn't a chance then, and gave it up, although his eyes suddenly showed a flame as sinister as that in Blood's orbs. The latter had seen his intent, and now he grinned at him.

"Don't be anxious," he whispered. "Your turn will come soon enough." Then he once more looked upwards where the macaw was now wheeling again, screaming at the men who were holding the boy on the cross-trees.

It did not take long to complete the work. The boy was secured to one end of the rope which had been passed through the block, his wrists being jerked high above his head, then, as they released him, his body swung free and they pulled on the rope until he had been hoisted about halfway up the fore topmast.

Then they secured the free end of the rope to the cross-trees, and for once the impassivity of the stern-faced man on the deck cracked as he saw the body of his young companion swing outward to the roll of the ship. Then it came back on the return roll, and, as it swung downward on the arc, it struck the foremast with terrific force and rebounded, spinning like a stuffed guy as it was jerked to the end of the arc.

Again it swung inwards with the roll of the ship, and again it banged against the foremast with sickening force as it passed. It was about the most devilish form of manhandling known on the high seas, and, although it has been indulged in at times, there have been few skippers with the nerve to face a crew and carry it out.

Watching, the other prisoner found himself fascinated in a horrible way. No human frame could withstand blow after blow like that. Bones must give and break and become mashed into the flesh. It was just a gamble how long the victim would remain conscious under the awful punishment—a torture as terrible as any rack ever devised by the Inquisition of old.

Whether Bully Blood intended that the boy should swing there until he was beaten to an unconscious pulp, or whether he meant to smash him just to a certain point, no one but Blood himself knew; and not until the body had spun and swung and banged a dozen times did he give a sign. And all that time the pink macaw had been wheeling about in a frenzy of rage, and what seemed like despair.

It was then that Blood gave a sign to the cabin boy who had re-loaded the shotgun, and, taking up the weapon, Blood called up to the victim of his devilry.

"That bird," he said, "that blanked bird —when it stops that racket and perches, you will be released. Give the sign, you scum!"

The purple lips of the boy moved in answer of some kind, but Blood could not hear from the deck, and called to the men in the cross-trees to pass on what had been said.

"He says he will see you drop dead first," came the answer.

"Then we'll see what a little more swinging will do," said Blood, still showing his teeth.

The body had already started again on the outward arc to starboard, and Blood was watching its progress, when several things took place which altered the whole position on the ship.

The first thing came when the stern-faced man, who, since his other brief struggle, had been standing quiescent, suddenly broke into action as if steel springs had been let loose.

With a jerk that brought him free for a moment, he sprang

forward; then, as two of his captors hurled themselves upon him, he brought up his arms and slammed their heads together with a force that could be heard all over the deck. They went down with skulls cracked like eggshells, and, as a third leaped upon him, the man shot his arms outward and upward, and his hands closed round the neck of his assailant.

What happened then no one rightly knew. He seemed to make a slight motion with his hands which flicked the head of the other first to one side, then to the other, and each time there was the sound of a slight "click." Then he released his hold, and the other slumped to the deck, his neck broken clean in two places.

With a whirl, the grave one was on the poop, and at the same moment there came a bright flash of pink and indigo as the big macaw shot down from above.

Blood tried to get a bead on the bird, but, before he could do so, the macaw was into his face, clawing and screaming, and as he backed away, dropping the gun to tear at the bird with his hands, the man who had sprung from the deck reached the weapon, and grabbing it up, swung just as the second mate rushed him. He pulled the trigger of one barrel while the gun was still against his hip, and the whole charge took the second mate full in the stomach.

On the deck, near where the cabin-boy was cowering, was a small canvas bag containing cartridges, which he had brought up with the gun, and this the man caught up as he sprang towards the rail. The Yankee mate was hesitating, and the men on the main deck were standing mouths agape at this sudden turn of affairs.

Up above, the body of the red-headed boy still swung back and forth, each time it passed the foremast striking with sickening force. But the pair on the cross-trees had no eyes for that now. They were watching the play of the drama beneath, and a general gasp went up as the man with the gun jammed the muzzle into Bully Blood's back, and cried a sharp command to the macaw.

The bird obeyed at once, and came to rest on his shoulder, while the man with the gun forced Blood along until he held him at one side of the poop, where he could command the whole deck.

"Get that man down—quick!" snarled the one who now held the command. "If he swings twice more, I'll give you the whole charge in the back! Quick, I say!"

And, lifting his livid countenance, Bully Blood called up to the two men on the cross-trees to catch the body as it swung and release it. They did so, and, when they had untied the wrists of the boy, who was now unconscious, they eased it down to the deck, where it slumped in a loose heap like an empty sack.

For the space of perhaps thirty seconds the man with the gun studied the situation, then his eyes sought the West, where the sun was already dipping beneath the horizon. Darkness, he knew, would be on them in half an hour, and as he realised this he seemed to make up his mind what he should do.

"A boat!" he said curtly. "Have a boat swung out, and two men told off to man the oars. I'm seeing that you do as I say, or you get this charge."

Blood glanced towards the Yankee mate, who was standing at the rail, watching the scene.

"Mister—" he began, dry-lipped.

But the man at his back cut him short.

"Give your own orders!" he snarled. "Never mind the mate—I'll look after him!"

So Blood whispered out a command for a boat to be lowered away, and for two men to get into it. Then the other told him to have the unconscious boy lowered gently into it, and this, too, was done. Then, while the violet wing in the East spread over the sky as the dusk deepened, the man with the gun stood motionless, watching until he judged the right moment to make the next move. Then he drove Blood before him, down from the poop and along the deck, until he was just above where the boat, rocked to the swell.

"That bird," he said quietly— "that bird, Blood—I heard the story of that bird from the man who gave it to the boy. You were right, Blood. It is the same macaw that gouged out your neck in the South Seas. Its owner was the same old man you manhandled as you did this boy to-day. The macaw knew you quick enough, Blood. But I didn't guess who you were until your fingers went to your throat, and I saw that scar under the left ear.

"There is a devil in that bird, Blood, and it will get you yet. That is why I am not going to kill you to-day. There is lots of time for that, but I'll get you, Blood, I'll get you somewhere, some time, when you least expect it. I'll give you plenty of rope for a while, Blood, but when you will fall hardest is when I'll strike.

"And the bird, Blood, the pink macaw, he will be alive then, and you'll feel his claws and his beak again, Blood. He's not a bird, Blood. He's a devil, and he hates you, Blood. Remember what I say, Blood; and some time, out of the night, I'll come!"

With that he tossed the bag of cartridges into the boat, and, still holding the shotgun ready, dropped down into the bow. The two sailors were seated at the oars ready, and he gave a curt command for them to give way.

As the boat slipped away from the schooner, he gazed up at Blood, who was standing at the side just where he had left him, and as he did so the latter opened his lips, and a stream of appalling curses came whispering through the growing dusk. But the man with the gun only laughed, and the pink macaw broke into another frenzy of screeches.

Then Blood disappeared, and, as if he guessed what it was about, the man with the gun urged on the oarsmen. That he had figured Blood's intention aright was proved a few moments later, when the crack of a revolver sounded on the deck of the schooner, and a bullet whistled overhead. It mattered not to Blood whether he hit his own men or not so long as he "got" the tall figure in the bow.

But although the lead plomped all about them, and once hit the gunwale, the man with the macaw still stood in laughing disdain until they were out of range. Then he sat down, and for the rest of the journey to the shore his gaze rested broodingly on the unconscious boy on the boards in the stern.

On reaching the shore, the man with the gun made the two sailors carry the boy ashore and lay him down on the grass under the trees; then he ordered them back to the schooner, and they had seen enough of him by then to obey without question.

When the boat had disappeared in the darkness, the man turned his attention to the unconscious boy, but it took him only a few minutes to realise that he was past all human aid. He sat beside him, and held him in his arms, and it was thus that the boy's spirit took flight, his life whispering away like a tiny breath. And it was then the man rose and solemnly consecrated himself to vengeance on Bully Blood, and if Blood had guessed for a single moment who it was that had taken command of his ship that day and had vowed to have his life he would have felt far more uneasy than was the case.

For the grave-faced man that took his way through the jungle that night, after burying the boy's body as well as was possible, was one who had been for twenty years on Devil's Island, the terrible French penal settlement off the coast of French Guiana, in South America, one who had been patrolled after that time in Cayenne, and had escaped across into British Guiana, had gone up to the unknown reaches of the Essequibo, and had come out of there with a fortune in diamonds, and now, with a letter of credit inside his shirt for close on a hundred thousand pounds, was bound north to the haunts of his early life, where he had been convicted of a crime which he had never committed.

He was a bitter man and a dangerous man, and Bully Blood could not have chosen a more deadly foe than the man who was known in the convict settlement on Devil's Island as the Black Eagle.

And with him went the pink macaw.

THE END OF THE PROLOGUE.

THE STORY.

PART ONE.

CHAPTER 1.   The History of the Gore Shipping Line.

NEVER in the history of shipping was there such a gigantic boom in the values of all forms of merchant craft as took place during the years of the Great War. The big combines had entire fleets taken over by their respective governments at figures which filled the souls of the shareholders with joy.

The smaller companies either shared this same delectable fate or else sold their ships, both in and out of commission, at fabulous prices.

Individual owners could command almost any price and any rate of charter for old hulks that, up to then, had been stuck in the mud on the edge of some boneyard.

From every creek and bay and estuary in the Americas and Europe, in Africa and Australia dilapidated old hookers of wood and iron were hauled out and put into commission and found eager buyers on every hand.

In those days, to own a ship, no matter what its condition, was to have a direct call on a fortune, and for four or five years the game went on merrily.

Hulks that had been passed over by ship-breakers, as not even worth smashing up for their metal, suddenly blossomed out in a new coat of paint, and once again wallowed groggily along the seas to which they had bade farewell years before.

Old wooden schooners, which would have been dear at a few hundred before the war, fetched thousands; and any man who could get his ship and cargo to a given destination was made for life. To do it twice meant real wealth, and half a dozen times was sufficient to put him high up among the magnates.

That was while the boom lasted; and there is many a man with wide country acres and a fleet of motor-cars to-day who, before the shipping boom, would have counted himself lucky to run to a tax twice a month before riches tumbled into his lap.

And, just as there are many like that, there are many more who rode fickle Lady Luck too long, and when the crash came, took the steep slide to ruin.

To-day one can see ships of every size and age and degree moored in rotting and rusty rows in every port of the world— grim witness of the awful world slump which struck practically without warning three years after the armistice. And there they are likely to remain, for not even the salvage companies will have anything to do with them.

Here and there a wholesale orgy is indulged in; and, just recently, nearly three hundred wooden ships, built during the war at top-of-the-crest cost of over sixty millions of pounds sterling, were bought by the salvage folk for less than sixty thousand pounds, and burned in one grand holocaust as the cheapest way of securing the metal in them!

And off one port on the west coast of America can be seen ninety-nine quite new destroyers lying in long, mournful-looking lines, out of commission, unwanted, and not even worth the trouble of breaking up.

But as has been said, there were those who started to ride the crest early in the game, and with the right hunch at the right time to cash in and pull out before the crash came. Some, there were, too, who sensed the right moment well enough but did not find it so easy to pull out as they thought, and, while some managed to do so, there were others who did not.

Now, among the men who were shrewd enough to see the crash coming, and who made strenuous efforts to realise and get out from under before the storm broke, was one, Captain Barnfield Gore who, at the commencement of the boom, had been skipper of his own ship, a dilapidated old hooker which was known all over the seven seas, and which, for many years, had gained for its owner a precarious but fairly steady income in many devious ways.

Captain Gore's other name was really Barney, but no one but himself could have told that, and generally, among sailor men high and low, he was known as Captain Bully Blood, with a reputation as bad as that of any man who ever sailed the seas.

A couple of cargoes—quite legitimate for a change— early in the war put a nice lump of money in Gore's pockets, and, with his weather eye a'cock, he sensed well enough what was due to happen in the shipping world as hostilities proceeded, and every available bottom was brought into commission to rush food cargoes to Europe.

Before that day actually arrived, Gore had purchased two other ships, and, with his fleet of three, they operated with considerable success for a couple of years or so. Whatever his faults, Gore was a first-class seaman, and cared not two straws for any man.

He was lucky enough to have skippers of his other two ships with about as much nerve as himself, and the result was that, in the space of a couple of years, Gore accumulated more wealth than he had ever conceived of in his wildest dreams.

And it was not very long before his ambition grew. He was a shipowner then— could even boast that he owned his own fleet. But that wasn't enough. He wanted to be ashore, in his own offices, with his own name on the ground-glass doors of a suite of offices, and, to add still further to the units of the Gore Line. Not an unnatural ambition, to be sure, but somewhat different from those which had formerly ruled in the mind of Bully Blood.

Still, it is extraordinary what changes come over some men when they suddenly find themselves dropped into the ranks of capitalists, and such changes have been known to cause the deepest red of communism to fade to a mild and innocuous pink.

At any rate, Captain Barnfield Gore, to give him his full legal appellation, carried out his intention, and, while the "going was still good," established himself in offices in Fenchurch Street, where the windows proclaimed that the Gore Shipping Line had its executive headquarters.

By that time Captain Gore—who was the sole owner of the Gore Line—had five ships —three sailing crafts and two iron tramps— which he valued at the time at no less than six hundred thousand pounds; and a couple of hundred thousand pounds in cash in bank and sound securities.

From this, it will be seen that he could consider himself a rich man, and as the wave was still rolling high, it looked as if a few more years of judicious juggling might make the Gore Line a really important company.

In his sea-going days, Gore had paid little attention to his personal appearance. His clothes had always been carelessly thrown on, and his strangely black beard had always appeared unkempt. But Gore had always possessed a very strong personality, and what would have seemed sloppy in a more ordinary man seemed not out of keeping with the dominating cold eyes, the strange uncanny whispering voice, and the ruthless fist of Bully Blood.

But as Captain Barnfield Gore, president and general manager of the Gore Shipping Line, all that was changed. He was turned out by one of the most exclusive tailors in Savile Row. His black beard was brought under control and trimmed to a neat black point. His manners were subdued, and patterned after those of other City men whom he studied. He made it a point to know only highly respectable and influential people, and through these it was not long before he belonged to a good lunch club in the City and an equally sedate social club in the West End.

He bought himself a small but extremely well-appointed house in Upper Brook Street, where he gave frequent dinners to business and social acquaintances; and no man dined there but voted Gore's chef fully deserving of the button of the famous Club des Cent, which, it is said, he possessed. He had a couple of good cars in his garage, and riding and driving horses in his stable.

He was generous to the call of charity, and particularly to those who made it a practice to publish the names of their subscribers, and so on, and so on.

From all of which, it will be seen that Captain Gore had established himself both in a business and social way, thanks to the wave of prosperity which struck the shipping world during the tight years of the war. And this was Gore's position at the time when that terrific cloud was gathering to carry ruin to the four quarters of the globe.

It was unperceived by the shrewdest men in the business and financial worlds. Those who actually saw it coming could be counted on the fingers of two hands. Generally it struck without warning, and, as everyone knows, vast fortunes were swept away in a few hours, a few days, a few weeks, or, at most, a few months.

Great firms wrote off millions, or went through drastic reconstruction. Smaller firms, and those without large reserves or sound credits, simply disappeared from the scheme of things. Others staggered along somehow, hoping that something would turn up, and so it went in England as elsewhere. And in no place did the slump strike harder than in the shipping world.

Captain Gore did not note the first mutterings of the storm. He was a good seaman, but there were many things about the intricacies of finance and business which he had not yet grasped; and hence it was that he was very greatly dependent on the guiding advice of his confidential manager.

Gore deemed himself peculiarly lucky in his choice of a manager. At first, when he had established himself ashore, he had thought to run his business with an ordinary staff with himself in direct control. Thus he had run his ship, and thus he thought he could steer through the shoals of the City.

But he soon found himself beyond his depth, and, while he hated to confess it, even to himself, he soon realised that he must have a competent manager who knew the finance and business game from A to Z, and whom he could trust.

Such a man had come to him at the very moment when he had made that decision. Gore had not advertised, and was under the impression from what the applicant said, that he had been sent along by some acquaintance to whom he must have mentioned that he was on the look-out for a good manager.

At any rate, Gore engaged him, and it was not long before he was congratulating himself on his perspicacity. Nor was it long before the new manager, David Burr by name, had got the actual strings of control into his own hands.

Gore supervised matters generally, and personally conducted the interviews with his various skippers, but it was Burr who made most of the cargo contracts, handled all questions of finance, supplies, and insurance, and kept the office staff working like a well-oiled machine.

Now, in order to understand how it was that certain very serious complications arose in the affairs of Captain Barnfield Gore (and which rose through a sequence of very strange incidents, to a climax of stark tragedy), it is necessary to take observation of the private and business lives of both Captain Gore and his confidential manager, David Burr, at a period of time some two months or so before the first rumblings were heard of the great slump which was even then forming.

And, since David Burr was a prime factor in those events, it is by an account of his movements at the time that a clear conception of the strange affair can be gained. Therefore, it will prove instructive to note the manager's actions on a certain evening about the time referred to.

On this day things had gone much as usual in the offices of the Gore Shipping Line. All five of the ships composing the Gore fleet were at sea with full cargoes, and wireless messages had been received stating that one of the iron tramps would make Cape Town the following day, while the second steam craft would dock at Liverpool that same evening.

The three sailing vessels had not been heard from, but there was no reason to fear that everything was not all right with them. One was somewhere on the China coast; a second was making the run home from the Plate; and the third was outward bound for 'Frisco with general cargo for that port, and the promise of a lucrative timber load for the return voyage.

So, all in all, everything was going quite as well as Captain Gore could have wished. He himself had left the office somewhat early on this particular afternoon of a grey winter day, but his manager was to be found at his desk until the departure of the last clerk. Then he, too, prepared to leave, and, from the manner in which he was greeted by the liftman as well as the porter on the ground floor, it was plain that the tall, grave-faced man was respected by, and popular with, those employees of the building.

In fact, although he ruled with a stern hand, David Burr was equally respected by the office staff, although no one ever dreamed of approaching him other than in the most formal manner. There was something in those deep-set, brooding eyes, in the cold abruptness of gesture and sombre reserve of manner, that forbade anything else; but the manager knew his job, and saw that every other employee knew his.

On this particular night, as he emerged into Fenchurch Street, he turned up the collar of his overcoat against the cold damp, and, joining the home-going crowds, made his way along to a bus stopping point. He swung aboard there and managed to get a seat up near the front, where he sat aloofly while the bus banged and jerked its way westward.

As it passed along High Holborn he rose and made his way to the rear platform, and when it stopped at Kingsway he dropped off.

He wended his way on foot up Southampton Row until he came to a public-house on one corner. He entered there, and, with a civil nod to the barmaid, who seemed to know him as a regular customer, he ordered a large whisky-and-soda, which he was accustomed to do at the same hour each evening in the same bar. He smoked a cigarette and consumed his drink leisurely; then, bidding the barmaid good-night, he left and once more started along on foot.

He turned to the left, and kept on until, he came into Bedford Square, from which he made his way into Russell Square, and there he mounted the steps of what one could guess without any great amount of deduction was a respectable boarding-house.

CHAPTER 2.　The Queer Movements of David Burr.

DAVID BURR let himself in by his own key, closing the door after him, stood for a few moments looking down the dimly lit hall. From up the basement stairs came the smell of cooking, and as the fumes assailed his nostrils the man made a slight moue of distaste. Then, with just the suggestion of a shrug, he strode to the stairs and began to mount.

On reaching the first floor he turned to the left and walked along the hall to a door which opened into a large bed-sitting-room furnished to a fair degree of comfort.

The blinds had been drawn and a cheerful fire was burning in the open grate. The maid had already brought a jug of hot water over which a clean white towel had been laid, and when he had thrown off his outer clothes, David Burr began his ablutions.

When he was finished and had resumed his coat, he seated himself before the fire, lit a cigarette, and perused an evening paper until he heard the sound of a gong somewhere below. He at once rose and tossed the paper on to the table. Then he left the room, and, as he descended the stairs, found himself one of several others who had appeared from other rooms.

He greeted them all courteously and joined in a discussion of the weather while they all entered a large dining-room on the ground floor where the evening meal was laid, and where a large, buxom-looking woman stood at the end of the table awaiting them.

David Burr was seated next to the hostess, and it was obvious from the way in which she addressed him, and the attention which she gave to any remark he made, that he was, unquestionably, the "star boarder," and from the attitude of the other boarders it was equally plain that they, too, deferred to him.

It was a mixed company, such as one finds in any house of the sort. Aside from Burr (whose position as managing clerk in the Gore Shipping Line was known) there were a couple of solicitor's clerks, who looked as if they would remain in that same position for the rest of their days. There was a young woman of abrupt manners who conducted a private typing bureau, and who confined her remarks chiefly to David Burr.

There was another young woman of cheerful round red countenance who was at the head of a department in one of the big shops in Oxford Street; a man who favoured garments of a horsey cut, and who, it was rumoured in the boarding-house, made his living on the 'Turf.'

There was a middle-aged man who was a solicitor in a small way of practise; another man also of middle age, who was a commission agent of sorts; and, finally, a lady of uncertain years who was supposed vaguely to be some sort of distant relative of the buxom woman who ran the place, and who apparently existed on a small annuity.

That made up the company, and it was here that David Burr would have been found at the same hour any evening during the eighteen months that had just gone by.

He was courteous and pleasant to all, but never did he mention business matters at the table, and there was something in the cold reserve of the man that prevented anyone from attempting to question him.

He was as "stand-offish" (as one of the young clerks put it) as he had been when he had first come to the place as a boarder; but, nevertheless, he was liked or, where he was not particularly liked, was at least respected, and no one would have dreamed of encroaching past the line of reserve he had set up.

When the meal was over he did not remain to gossip, as did some of the others, but rose at once, and, with a bow to first his hostess, then the other ladies at the table, and, finally, the men, he left the room, and they heard him mounting the stairs.

It was generally supposed that Mr. Burr belonged to a modest club to which he repaired each evening, but no one, not even his hostess, knew at what hour he returned.

On this evening he did not go out at once, but first smoked a cigarette in front of the fire and resumed his perusal of the evening paper in which he seemed to find considerable interest. Had one been bending over his shoulder, one might have seen that the article which held his attention was one dealing with the sudden decline in shipping values, and the wholesale cutting in marine freight rates which was taking place all over the world.

David Burr had followed this movement for some time past, and through the information which came through the Gore offices, had watched every phase of the matter like a hawk; but he took care to read every item touching on the subject, and perhaps his enhanced interest in the article he was reading can be better understood when it is disclosed that it was he himself who had written it, and submitted it to the journal in question.

In fact, there were quite a few rumours in the shipping world which had been inspired at the same source, but the last person to suspect that would have been Captain Barnfield Gore.

It was getting on for nine o'clock when he laid his paper aside and rose. He put some fresh fuel on the fire, then he got into his overcoat and hat and turned out the light.

He saw a couple of the other boarders in the lower hall as he went out and gave them a curt nod. He knew that, as the door closed after him, they were saying that Mr. Burr was going to his club, and that was exactly what he wanted them to think and to say.

From the square he made his way on foot to High Holborn, and there he boarded a bus that would take him to the Marble Arch. He descended at that well-known point and took his way on foot along Edgware Road.

He continued along this until he came to a side street on the left which led into a secluded crescent. He walked half-way round this crescent until he came to a corner, where he turned off.

On that corner was a narrow old-fashioned house, which residents of the crescent remembered as having belonged to a famous but eccentric artist. He had built it according to some fantastic ideas of his own away back in the sixties of last century, and, owing to its bizarre interior plan, it had lain empty for several years after his death.

Unlike the other houses in the crescent, it had no front door. Where that useful portal should have been was just a blank wall, and, high up in the wall, a wide, bowed glass front that gave light to a vast studio.

The only visible entrance was in the side wall round the corner, and those who had ever entered the house knew that from this entrance a staircase led to the living apartments on the first floor, back of the studio.

On the ground floor was an extraordinary sort of apartment which, in the old days, had been fitted up as a Shanghai poppy den, and rumour had it that the young bucks of the 'sixties' and 'seventies' had staged some wild orgies there.

Back of this place were domestic offices and a kitchen, and

beyond that again a small garden shut off from the view of its neighbours by a very high wall, which had once been the subject of litigation.

The living quarters above on the first floor were extremely luxurious, and the place had never been furnished more sumptuously than at the present time. Bizarre as the plan of the building was, it was an ideal place for a bachelor who might be an artist, and, from the appearance of the interior at this time, the present tenant appeared to be both. For the tenant was none other than David Burr, confidential clerk to Captain Barnfield Gore, of the Gore Shipping Line, and star boarder at the boarding-house already referred to in Russell Square. He had purchased the lease some time before the opening of this story, and, among those who had taken any note at all of the new occupant, it was understood vaguely that he was a wealthy gentleman who had returned to England after spending many years abroad pursuing his art.

No one had entered the house—or been permitted to enter—to inspect whatever examples of his art which he may have brought back with him; but, had they done so, they would have found some extremely well-executed paintings hanging on the walls of the various rooms and in the studio.

But those paintings were not signed with the name of David Burr, for it was not by that name the tenant of the house was known. The name of the purchaser of the lease had been given as David Stone, and this, too, was the name signed to the various paintings. And certainly no one dreamed of connecting David Stone with the clerk in the shipping offices in the City.

One might have gained some hint of what part of the world the artist had visited during his absence from England, for nearly all the subjects were of a tropical nature in which the artist had seemed to catch the very spirit of the white surf, the green palms, and the blue sea.

And it was to this house David Burr made his way on the cold, damp night in question.

He fitted a key into the side door and let himself in. As he closed the door after him he stood just inside for a few seconds gazing about him at the beautifully furnished lounge hall.

On the floor were Eastern rugs, while luxurious silk-covered divans had been placed in two corners. From the centre of the ceiling was suspended a magnificent copper filigree brazier, in which a softened light was burning. The walls were lined with rare old tapestries and silks.

When he had finished his inspection the man drew a deep breath, like one who has been under water a considerable time. Then he walked across to a small rosewood tabourette and took up a small silver bell. He rang it gently, and set it down.

Almost immediately there came a sound from the direction of the staircase, and a moment later there appeared a very strange figure.

He was dressed in the regulation black of the servant, but his walk was more the roll of an old sailor than of the landsman. His face was literally pitted with smallpox scars, and his colour, accentuated in that subdued light, was of a deep coppery hue. His eyes were of a queer shade of yellow, and absolutely expressionless. His nose was twisted and flattened as if it had been smashed half a dozen times. His hair grew low on his forehead, and was beginning to show streaks of grey against the black. One of his ears held a big gold earring in the lobe. The other ear was "cauliflowered," and, at one time, the earring which had decorated it had evidently been dragged out by force, for the lobe was torn and hung loose. His body was heavy and squat, his shoulders broad, and the "barrel" of his body enormous. His arms were exceptionally long, and swung, apelike. In brute strength he appeared far above the ordinary; in mental capacity he would scarcely have passed the "twelve-year-old test."

The man who had entered stood by the tabourette waiting for the other to approach. As he approached him he did a strange thing for one who was so obviously the master. He lifted his arm and laid it across the heavy shoulders of the servant, then he patted his arm in an affectionate manner. But the words he spoke were even more strange than his actions.

"Well, brother mine," he said, in tones that were almost as tender as those of a woman, "is all well with thee?"

The dull eyes of the misshapen creature lightened at the touch and the tone. His mouth opened in what was evidently meant for a smile, exhibiting big, crooked, yellow teeth. There was not one feature about that poor bit of humanity that Nature had not mocked in the beginning and man had not accentuated in brute treatment— except one thing, and that was his voice.

It was the purest, sweetest voice that ever issued from the throat of man—vibrant and clear as a golden bell, flexible as the "voice" of a Stradivarius under the touch of the maestro.

"It is long since thou hast come, dear brother," he said, fondling the thin, supple hand of the one who was such a physical contrast to himself. "What hast thou brought me?"

"Ah, moi petit, see what I have brought thee this time!"

With that the speaker thrust a hand inside his coat and took out a small packet wrapped in tissue paper. He gave it to his brother—for the term used between them was no formal expression, but indicated their exact relationship, children of the same mother—and stood back while the other opened it.

A few moments later there was revealed a small bit of ivory carved in the form of a full-rigged ship, perfect in every last detail. The great hairy hands of the deformed one came up, holding the carving with infinite gentleness.

He devoured it with his eyes, and his voice came in a cry of utter joy as he pressed it to his lips. His strange eyes burned with an extraordinary light as they flashed at his brother, then he turned and sped up the staircase to disappear from view.

The man by the tabourette watched him disappear, then with a heavy sigh he threw his overcoat and hat aside and opened a silver cigarette box. He lit a choice A-Batschari, and sinking into a low club chair, fixed his eyes on the copper brazier overhead.

He was thinking—thinking of what had filled the past two years; thinking of what had gone those twenty years before, during which he was as completely out of the world as if he had been entombed.

For the history of those twenty years had been as terrible to the man who now called himself David Stone in that bizarre house, and David Burr in the City, as a Monte Cristo or a Jean Valjean had known; and at the end of all his own suffering he had returned to find in his afflicted brother something which was more like the hunchback of a Hugo than flesh and blood of his own.

CHAPTER 3.　The Life Story and Resolve of the Black Eagle.

A LITTLE more than twenty years before, a young English art student had appeared in the Latin Quarter of Paris, where he was soon an intimate member of a small coterie of other students who were not giving very serious attention to their art studies. In fact, they spent most of their nights in dissipation, and their days in sleeping off the effects, and it was not long before the young student, John Hasford, by name, had adopted their mode of life.

With these wild blades, he spent most of his time until, at the end of a year, something happened which hurled him from the careless, happy-go-lucky life of the Quarter into the worst living hell on earth.

It was one night after he and his friends had been through a solid week of debauch that things reached a climax for John Hasford. More than twenty years were to go by before the whole truth came out of what happened that tragic night, but, at the time, it was John Hasford who was made the victim; and, since it was John Hasford who reappeared in the world twenty years later as David Stone, it will be as well to describe what took place.

The crowd with which he had been associating had, as had been stated, been on a wild debauch for a week, and on one night wound up at a cafe in the Boul' Mich' for supper. After this, all hands adjourned to the rooms of one of the gang to play cards—someone had dug up a faro outfit somewhere, and at the time the game was the craze in the Latin Quarter.

In addition to the men, there were two girls present—models—and they, too, took a hand in the game.

No one could have told how long the play continued before a dispute started, for all hands were drinking steadily, but it was sometime in the early hours of the morning. Everyone took a hand in the row, including the two girls, and the place was pretty badly smashed up.

Following this, peace of a sort was restored, and some of the cooler heads took themselves off. A few remained—five men and the two girls. The play was restarted, but, before long, another row broke out and that broke up the game entirely.

Now, at that point the stories which were told later showed great disagreement. Some of the men said they had departed immediately after the second row, leaving the host alone. Others could not remember just what had followed.

But the next day the news was soon over the Quarter that one of the five men who had remained after the first row—John Hasford, to be exact—had been arrested during the morning, charged with the murder of a model, one, Helene Merchardier, who was one of the girls present at the party, and, in fact, the one about whom both rows had started.

She had been John Hasford's model for some time, and it had been rumoured that the two were to be married soon. Hasford had been the host, and the story was that, about ten o'clock in the morning, the concierge of the building had entered his sitting-room to find him lying across the table asleep among the litter of cards and bottles and glasses, and, on the floor near him, was Helene Merchardier.

She was dead, had been shot through the heart, and, just underneath Hasford's right hand was a nickel-plated revolver, which was his own property. The concierge informed the police, and Hasford awoke to find himself charged with murder.

The trial was one of the sensations of Paris at the time, and, on the evidence, John Hasford was sentenced to life imprisonment on Devil's Island, the terrible French penal settlement off the coast of French Guiana in South America.

But John Hasford had never fired the shot that killed Helene Merchardier. Nor was the shot fired by one of the other four men present, when the second row started. But among that quartette was a scheming Judas who swore John Hasford to his doom, and for twenty years he existed as a numbered unit on Devil's Island.

The day was to come when the mystery of that tragic night was to be cleared up, but not until John Hasford had escaped from Cayenne, on the mainland, where he had been paroled after twenty years, and, after plunging into the wild jungles of British Guiana, just over the border, had emerged with a fortune in diamonds, and a terrible vow to wreak vengeance on each of the five men whose evidence had sent him to that hell.

So John Hasford had come back to Europe, but he had not reached London without putting his purpose into execution, and on the way had sought out and killed one of the five, who was then a prosperous merchant in the city of Havana, in Cuba; had next tracked down a second, who was then a New York banker, and had killed him.

Then in London he had killed a third, and it was on this occasion, about two years before the opening of the present story, that, the famous criminologist Sexton Blake, who had had the investigation in hand, had ferreted out the truth about John Hasford.

In Hasford's dossier at the Prefecture of Police in Paris, which covered every moment of Hasford's life from the moment of his arrest, twenty odd years before, to the time of his escape from Cayenne, Sexton Blake had learned more than a little about the man.

For instance, he had made a close study of the convict's daily life; had taken careful note of the hobbies he had been permitted to follow after ten years' confinement. Sexton Blake knew that the convict had displayed no little talent as a painter, and had made himself more than ordinarily proficient as a cabinet-maker in fine woods, and a carver in wood and ivory.

And, above all, the detective had observed in the dossier that John Hasford had consistently practised such exercises as would develop the muscles of the wrists and arms to an extraordinary degree, so much so, in fact, that, owing to his feats of strength from great heights, he had been christened by the other convicts, the Black Eagle.

And it was due to an unwitting display of that same strength of the hands on a certain occasion, that Sexton Blake had gained his first clue in the case on which he had been engaged—the clue which had brought him at length into direct contact with the Black Eagle.

And this man, David Stone, of the strange house in the crescent off the Edgware Road —the man who was confidential clerk to Barnfield Gore—sometime "Bully Blood" of the Seven Seas—the man who had filled other queer roles as well, was the same Black Eagle; and Sexton Blake at least would have had strong suspicions that the Black Eagle would not toil for months as an ordinary clerk in the City unless he had some strong motive for doing so. But not even Blake knew of a certain incident which had taken place when the Black Eagle was on his way north from South America after his escape from the French colony, and his clean-up in diamonds in the jungles of British Guiana.

It was an interlude, so to say, between the time of his escape and the killing of the merchant in Havana, and only the Black Eagle himself knew of the vow he had made that, one day, be it in the near or distant future, he would exact full payment from the notorious "Bully Blood" for his brutal treatment of the red-headed lad who had been his companion on that journey northward on the occasion when Blood had become insanely angered at sight of the pink macaw, and had had the youth pounded to a pulp against the fore topmast of his schooner.

The Black Eagle had not known the whole story of the pink macaw at that time. It was only from a few things that the boy had told him before he died that same night, and which the Black Eagle had finally been able to piece together into a coherent whole, that he had guessed the truth. Slowly but surely, he had traced the history of the macaw.

There are men who say that a special devil lives in every giant pink macaw, for they are as rare as albinos among men, and there is something uncanny and strange about them that has always roused the superstitious instincts of the ordinary sailor man.

That it had not been the first time "Bully Blood" had seen that same macaw the Black Eagle now knew. The bird was as much of a sea rover as Blood himself. At the time it must have been nearly twenty years old, and it was all of ten years before that incident, off the coast of the Spanish Main, that Blood and the pink macaw had clashed in the South Pacific.

Blood might violate every rule of high heaven and man, but deep within him was the same streak of superstition which lives in most men who go down to the sea in ships, and, within that bundle of pink and indigo plumage he firmly believed that the curse which had been laid upon him in those years agone still lived to become his undoing if he gave it a chance.

All this, and more, the Black Eagle ferreted out; and when he had rounded off the story he had set out to exact pay merit from "Bully Blood."

But the man was no longer "Bully Blood" of the Seven Seas. As the reader of this record already knows, prosperity had overtaken him during the war when shipping values hit the sky, and it was as Captain Barnfield Gore of the young but growing and prosperous Gore Shipping Line that the Black Eagle had found him.

So much for that phase of it, which is essential to what followed swiftly on the heels of that drear night in autumn when the Black Eagle once more returned to his house in the crescent off the Edgware

Road.

When he finally managed to escape from the last tentacles of the hell-hole known as Devil's Island, the Black Eagle had been filled with but one dominating thought—to secure sufficient riches to make himself independent, and then to seek out, one by one, the men who, he believed, had betrayed him twenty years before in Paris, and to kill each.

The incident which had taken place on "Bully Blood's" ship off the coast of the Spanish Main had been the first thing to jerk his mind round to the contemplation of something not immediately concerning himself, and he still had time to register a vow of vengeance on behalf of the boy who had been so foully murdered.

But it was not until he had reached England, and, after long search, had eventually found his brother, that he was seized by something which submerged even his own ego—no small thing when one remembers that for twenty years he had lived a completely introspective existence, feeding on the single thought of vengeance for his own wrongs.

His eyes had been appalled and the innermost chords of his soul wrung at that first meeting with his brother after the long passage of years. It was then twenty-five years since they had parted, and while Nature, at the beginning, had mocked Stephen Hasford, had made of him but the caricature of a human being, he had not been repulsively misshapen and brutally twisted as now.

No one but those two would ever know just what passed at that meeting. But for the first time since he had stood at his mother's knee John Hasford had wept, and in the awful contemplation of the terrible treatment Fate had meted out to his brother, he had, for a time, almost forgotten his own wrongs. Twenty-five years before, Stephen Hasford had been misshapen and simple of mind. But he had been passably capable, and when he had run away to sea had soon developed into a valuable and faithful servant of that exacting master.

But the same malignant spirit of evil that seemed fated to follow both the brothers had thrown Stephen Hasford into the hold of a hell-ship as bad as that of "Bully Blood," and away in the whaling grounds of the South Atlantic the man had been beaten and hammered, hammered and beaten, until what had been simple deformity was changed into the grotesque, ape-like creature John Hasford had found in his return from Devil's Island.

John Hasford had taken his brother to his arms and under his care. He was as gentle with him as a woman to her firstborn, and, in return, every conscious thought of the other was lavished on his protector.

Riches could not have bought the faithful and loving servitude which Stephen Hasford insisted on giving. He was supremely happy in his simple way just to dwell in the house of his brother, ready to serve him whenever he should return, delighted as a child with each new carved toy which the other never failed to bring (for the soul of the misshapen one was that of an artist, and carvings were his delight), and ready at any time to carry out any command which it might please his brother to give him, be it the fetching of a match or the killing of an emperor.

And in the calendar of vengeance which John Hasford had drawn up, there was a heavy red line under the name of the bucko skipper who had made of his brother what he found. That skipper was not "Bully Blood," and it was not fated to be John Hasford's hands which were to wring his neck for him. Fate was to place that vengeance in the power of the broken victim himself.

But it was after discovering what had happened to his brother that the Black Eagle had grown more determined than ever to sweep from the sea every bucko skipper and mate on whom he could lay his hands, and, discovering the new role of "Bully Blood," he had determined to begin with him.

Hence, it is that we find him serving the whilom skipper as confidential clerk, biding his time to strike; and be sure that Captain Barnfield Gore did not suspect for a single moment that the silent and efficient man who served him so well was the same sombre-faced individual who had backed him down on his own deck off the coast of the Spanish Main some years before. And far less did he guess that David Burr was none other than the deadly Black Eagle, who would kill his man with as little hesitation as he would snuff out the life of a mosquito.

Thus we find the position of the chief actors in this drama on the evening when the Black Eagle returned to his house in the crescent off the Edgware Road, for he had made up his mind that, at last, the time had come to strike down Barney Gore, alias Bully Blood.

Not that this was the first time he had returned recently. On the contrary. It had been his practise for some weeks past to come to the crescent not less than two evenings each week, for he had been slowly evolving things as he wished them to be when the time came to strike.

How he had succeeded in doing so will soon be seen, and there is not the slightest doubt that the very careful plans he had laid for the complete discrediting of Captain Barnfield Gore and his final annihilation would have marched without the least suspicion of foul play leaking out, had it not been his practise for some weeks past to things of a human factor on which the Black Eagle had not counted.

That human factor was Sexton Blake.

CHAPTER 4.   The Masked Gamblers.

FOR upwards of half an hour the Black Eagle sat alone, thinking about the past and the present. In that time he smoked several of the fragrant A-Batscharis, and it was only when he heard the faint tinkle of a gong somewhere above that he tossed away the fag end of a weed and rose.

He mounted to the floor above, and entered a luxuriously-furnished sitting-room. He kept on through it to a big bed-room beyond. Through a half-open door one could glimpse the gleaming white tiles of a bath-room, and, at the moment, the pleasant sound of running water could be heard.

The Black Eagle proceeded to undress. His movements were abrupt and precise, like those of one who had done a certain thing at a certain time each day for many years. Muscular habit is the hardest thing in the world to break. And, considering the harsh discipline of his life on Devil's Island for those terrible twenty years, it is little wonder that his movements should have become almost like those of an automaton.

When he was stripped, he threw on an Oriental silk dressing-gown and entered the bath-room. It was a magnificent apartment, built by the eccentric artist, but modernised by the present tenant. It had a huge sunk bath, the fittings of which were solid silver, as were those of the hand-basin. Mirrors almost covered two walls, while in one corner there was a wide basin set in the floor and, above, a complicated-looking array of silver taps for a shower.

Close to the edge of the sunk bath was a low, white enamelled chair, on which lay several big Turkish towels, and bending over the bath, testing the water with a thermometer, was the misshapen creature whom the Black Eagle called "brother."

The Black Eagle walked to the hand-basin which had already been half-filled in readiness. On a glass shelf above were all the implements for shaving, and the man made a quick but efficient job of that part of his toilet. He finished at just about the moment his brother rose from beside the bath with the brief remark that it was ready. Then the other plunged in, and for a quarter of an hour revelled in the hot, soothing water.

From that he went to the cold shower, after which he took a brisk rub down.

By the time he re-entered the bed-room his brother had laid out his clothes, and when he had finished he stood before the mirror with a critical frown on his face.

In full evening-dress, he did not bear much general resemblance to David Burr, the City clerk, but even so, he had good reasons that no one should have the slightest suspicion that he and David Burr were one and the same person, and he had planned ample security against discovery, as shall presently be seen.

On the dressing-table had been laid ready, a gold cigarette-case filled with his favourite cigarettes, a small gold pencil, a silk notecase, which bulged as if it had been stuffed to its capacity with banknotes—which it had been—a very thin platinum watch to which was attached a black silk fob, a small gold matchbox, a bunch of keys, a crocodile cigar-case, a thin gold tablet containing a small pad for memoranda, and a bit of folded black silk which looked as if it might be a mask—which, indeed, it was.

And it was this latter article in which the Black Eagle counted to secure his features from discovery.

He distributed these articles among various pockets, donned the mask, and, picking up a loose cigarette, bent over towards the flame of the match which his brother held out to him. Then he turned and led the way from the bed-room into the hall, and along this until he came to two doors —one at the very end of the passage, and the other immediately on the right close to it.

He turned the handle of the latter, and pushed the door open, disclosing a small, square apartment almost devoid of furniture. In one corner was burning a heavily-shaded electric light, and in another stood a high wooden stand on which rested a large heavy wire cage. Close to this was a second wooden stand, at the top of which was a plain, round, thick wooden perch.

There was one window in the room, the upper half of which was open, and, as he noticed that the door of the cage was also open, the Black Eagle turned quickly to his brother.

"Has Jacko not returned yet?" he asked.

"No, brother mine," answered the other. "he flew away at the usual hour this evening, but did not return at dusk as usual. He should have been back some time ago. But be not alarmed—he will come back in his own good time. He will take no chances of being seen or hurt."

The Black Eagle shook his head, and, walking to the window, drew the upper half of the sash still lower. He peered out into the thick, gloomy night, then he said:

"I suppose he will be all right. I think Jacko is as human as you or I, and he should know how to take care of himself by now. Still, it is very late, brother, and it is a drear night. It would be serious if anything has happened to him. Has the window been open all the time?"

"Every moment since he left," replied the deformed one. "I opened it and watched him go. I am sure he is all right. He will return presently safe and sound, as you will see."

"I hope so," remarked the Black Eagle as he turned away. "During the evening it will be well if you come here as often as possible to see if he is back, brother. And now, let us have a look at the studio—my guests will be arriving soon."

With that he crossed the room and stepped into the hall. When his brother had closed the door, the Black Eagle opened the other one and stepped out on to a gallery which ran all the way round the four walls of the great studio to which reference has already been made. He stood looking down where the easels and canvases and draperies had been pushed to one side in order to make room for a large oval-shaped table which had been covered with green baize.

It was directly under the great central chandelier, and around it were ten chairs— nine of an ordinary type and the tenth, placed half-way down one side, about six inches higher in the seat than the others.

Even from the galley it could be seen that the green baize was relieved by heavy gilt lines of a definite pattern, and, indeed, the oval of the table had been sub-divided into ten different sections, one being blank and directly in front of the high chair, and the others being numbered in gilt from one to nine.

In the centre of the table was a sort of box, nickel-fitted and sloping from the back to the front. It was a foot or so in length, and something under three inches in width and depth. The initiated would have recognised the table and appurtenances as a baccarat table and "shoe" ready for play, which was just what it was.

At one side was a large mahogany buffet on which stood several covered silver dishes, and close to that a smaller buffet on which reposed a number of bottles containing liquids of various colours, while on the floor were half a dozen champagne buckets each with its bottle and complement of ice.

It was evident that the Black Eagle was expecting company, and had made ample preparation for entertaining them.

He laid an affectionate hand on his brother's shoulders as he congratulated him on the arrangements, then he led the way back along the hall and down the stairs to the lounge on the ground floor. He glanced at a very old Egyptian water-clock then, noticing that it lacked just ten minutes of midnight, he turned once more to his brother.

For a full minute or so the two gazed in silence at each other, then the Black Eagle spoke, his voice low and almost toneless.

"To-night is the night, brother mine," he said slowly. "Things are now at the point where I shall become more active. Gore is becoming aware that things are going to be bad in the shipping world. And he must not get the chance to take his own head. So—to-night, little brother, it is to act. He will come with the others. At the right moment I shall give you the sign. And then the drop, brother, the drop which will place him in our power, the single drop which will course through his blood and turn it to water, the potion which will leave him at my mercy. Is it understood, brother?"

"It is understood," came the vibrant voice of the other. "I shall be on the alert, my brother. At the right moment I shall not fail. And then I know thou wilt be avenged."

"Fear not," responded the Black Eagle grimly. "I shall be avenged. And now make ready to receive our guests, brother. The hour is at hand."

It was sharp on the stroke of midnight when the low buzz of a concealed bell sounded, and the hunchback, in his guise of servant, passed from the lounge hall into the vestibule and opened the door by which the Black Eagle had entered the house.

In the meantime, the Black Eagle had risen and was standing with his back to a cheerful fire which was burning in the lounge, and thus the first two of his guests —masked liked himself—found him.

There was no greeting beyond a formal bow, and, as if understanding that there were others still to come, the two masked new arrivals handed their evening coats and silk hats to the "servant," who carried them away.

Then they helped themselves to a cigarette each, and bowed their thanks as their host indicated a couple of low club chairs. Just then the bell went again, and once more two masked gentlemen, in evening dress, were admitted.

On this occasion, however, the greetings were not entirely silent as before, for one of the newcomers crossed the lounge, and, with a brief nod at the two who were seated, approached the host who was again standing in front of the open fire.

"Nine and eight and the eight of nine," he said in a low voice, at which the host nodded, for those words were the correct pass phrase of the evening. Then he went on:

"I have brought with me a guest this evening. He is trustworthy, and as one of our number will be unable to come on account of illness I took the liberty of filling his place."

The Black Eagle nodded.

"The gentleman is welcome if you vouch for him," he said, and gave a bow in the direction of the one who had been the subject of the low-voiced conversation. Then the two last arrivals doffed their coats and hats, and they were still so occupied when the bell again rang. This time three men came in together and, almost on their heels, a fourth.

And as the last one crossed the threshold the hunchback closed and bolted the door, for they were now nine and the party was complete.

The host waited until the quartette had disposed of their hats and coats, then, with a slight gesture of the hand, he led the way in the direction of a door at the end of the lounge.

He opened this and ushered his guests into the studio where each one selected a chair at the baccarat table and seated himself.

The hunchback followed the others, and, after taking a lacquered box from a cupboard in one of the sideboards, seated himself at the table in the high chair, for it was he who acted the part of croupier on these occasions.

And here it should be explained that these baccarat parties were a regular weekly feature at the house of David Stone. The guests were composed of certain members of a private gambling club in Dover Street. This club had been closed some months before after the receipt of a tip from Sexton Blake (one of the members) that it would be wise to suspend operations for the time being.

That secret gambling club in Dover Street was but one of the many queer haunts to which Sexton Blake had the entree, and he was usually to be found from time to time at one or another for the simple reason that to keep in touch with the habitues of such places was part and parcel of his profession.

More than once his knowledge of the inner workings of the secret haunts of London and other great cities had proved invaluable to him in an inquiry, and it goes to show in what estimation he was held that never for a single moment did the directors of those places feel the slightest doubt of Blake.

It was not Blake's province to act as a "nark" for the police, and, indeed, he would have been sorry in many ways to see those various haunts wiped out, for their passing would break an important link between him and the Secret night life of the great capitals of the world.

He had been aware that, after the temporary closing of the club in Dover Street, several private little coteries had made it a practice of meeting at various private residences to continue to game until the club in Dover Street should be reopened.

But as he had taken little personal interest in these, he had been unaware until that very afternoon that one of these meeting places was the house in the crescent off the Edgware Road.

Blake had been distinctly curious to know how the Black Eagle had been putting in his time since his first meeting with that individual (when he had discovered his secret), and he had quickly seized on the chance to accompany one of that particular circle to the place when it was suggested that he should go along.

It was Sexton Blake who was the extra guest that evening, but, although the Black Eagle had peered at him closely, he had been unable to guess the identity of the person whose face was almost covered by the black silk mask which he wore, and, as it was a strict rule that no names should be mentioned, he could not, of course, ask any questions either directly of the new player or the gentleman who had brought him along.

As for Sexton Blake, he guessed, as little as did the Black Eagle, that a very curious thing was to occur before that game should finish, and, even if he had known that a certain Captain Barnfield Gore was one of the company, he would have thought nothing of it, for he had not even heard of Captain Gore, although he had heard of the notorious Bully Blood.

Nor did Blake know that the Black Eagle had planned for a long time to bring Captain Gore into that private circle, and that this was the fourth occasion on which Gore had visited the place, little dreaming that his wealthy and distinguished-looking host was his own clerk, David Burr!

CHAPTER 5.   The Game of Baccarat—And a Dramatic Interruption.

AS soon as the hunchback had settled himself in the high chair, and had dumped out a big pile of ivory chips from the lacquered box, the nine men in the players' seats drew out their wallets and began abstracting bundles of crisp bank-notes of a high denomination, for, like the stakes at the gambling club in Dover Street, the play in this private circle was of a very high order.

Deftly, despite the clumsy appearance of his big, misshapen hands and long, ape-like arms, the Black Eagle's brother set out the chips in nine lots containing three piles each, each pile of a different colour.

Those representing five pounds were red, those of twenty pounds green, and those of a hundred pounds each were blue in colour. There were none of less value than one pound.

Each lot of three piles contained twenty of the five-pound values, twenty of the twenty pounds, and five of the hundred-pound colour, making a total for each man of one thousand pounds, which gives some indication of the size of the game.

In exchange for the chips each handed over a bundle of notes in payment, and these the croupier thrust into the now empty lacquered box.

The Black Eagle, although the host, had bought chips just as the others, for in this game there was no "bank," each played standing an equal chance.

Then, when all was ready, the croupier took hold of the "shoe" — the box containing the six packs of mixed cards which make up the "shoe" in baccarat—and with a slight tap on the table indicated that he would make the first bank by auction.

From different parts of the table came low-voiced bids, someone beginning with fifty pounds—the minimum allowed in this game— and others running it up rapidly, until it had hit four hundred pounds, and at that figure the "shoe" was pushed across to the last bidder—a stout, masked gentleman, whose identity neither the Black Eagle nor Sexton Blake knew, although the latter had a suspicion that he would be able to identify him as a certain well-known sporting peer if he had found it necessary to do so.

This player thrust across four of the blue chips as his bank, and the hunchback placed them in front of him; then the latter took up his long "rake" and called the size of the bank. The player at Number One seat, whose first privilege it was to call the bank, said nothing, nor did the player at Number Two. But the one at Number Three called "banco," indicating that he was prepared to stake the sum of the bank against the one who held the "shoe," and when he had pushed four of the blue chips in front of him the one holding the "shoe" began to draw.

He pushed the first card, face down, across towards the croupier, keeping the second for himself; then the third, face down again, towards the croupier, and the fourth to himself. That was the first draw, and, picking up the two cards on the flat face of the "rake," the croupier tossed them across to Number Three, who had gone "banco." This player looked at them, taking care that the player holding the "shoe" could not see them, and, evidently thinking he could better his draw, exercised his privilege, and called for one more card.

At this his opponent, who until then had allowed his cards to remain face down, took a surreptitious look at his own cards, and then turned them over, revealing that he had drawn a face card—which counted ten— and a six. He then drew one more card from the "shoe," which he threw across face up to Number Three, and then, after a moment's hesitation, took a card for himself.

On being laid on the table, it proved to be a two-spot, which, with his six, made his total eight—a very useful number in baccarat, considering that it can only be beaten by nine.

Then, and then only, did Number Three show the two cards he still held in his hand. They were a ten and a four, and since the card which he had drawn was a five and the ten did not count, he had made a nine, which gave him the bank.

In that turn he had won exactly four hundred pounds, and now the shoe passed to the player next to the one who had just held it. That player was Sexton Blake, and since the "shoe" had been passed in routine form, there was no need to buy it this time by auction.

Blake started his bank with a single one hundred pound chip, and there were several calls of "banco." But it was the privilege of the previous man who had backed the bank to continue if he desired, and in this case Number Three chose to do so. So, after pushing a chip for a hundred out in front of him, Blake began to draw.

There is no need to go into details of every turn of the game that evening, but on this occasion Blake made four turns of his bank without losing, which means to say that he won his first turn, which left two hundred pounds in his bank; then on this he won the second turn, which made his bank four hundred; a third time he rode his "shoe," and again he won, making the amount in the bank eight hundred pounds. This was called by two players in partnership, and for the fourth time Blake won the turn, tieing with a nine twice before beating a seven with an eight on the third turn.

With his original hundred pound bank, he had run his winnings up to sixteen hundred pounds, and as Sexton Blake was one of the cold-blooded players who did not believe in riding his bank more than four turns unless under very exceptional circumstances, he now indicated that he would pass the "shoe," and at this the croupier pushed the pile of chips across the table with the "rake."

And so it went. One of the most consistent callers of "banco" was a black-bearded masked man, who sat in seat Number Five, and, as he took things leisurely, Sexton Blake noticed that he was playing what he would term a wild game, and was losing very large sums. Blake had seen him buy chips no less than three times since sitting down, which meant that he had run his losses into something over three thousand pounds in a little over an hour; but that would not matter much if he could get one good turn at the "shoe," for if he rode his bank, and passed the "shoe" while still winning, it would not take him long to cover his losses and show a balance to the good. It is just there that baccarat holds such a deep attraction for the big gambler, and after it even roulette hold's little attraction for him.

There was one other, too, who took note of the bearded man's losses, and that was the host, who was seated at Number Nine, just on the left of the croupier. He had taken the seat opposite on entering, but at request had changed with the player who had sat there.

The play proceeded with the usual ups and downs until two o'clock, when the host made a sign that they would stop for a little while for refreshments.

Of the nine players, the one at Number Three was still running on a winning streak; Blake was over two thousand ahead; the Black Eagle was winning by a few hundreds; and the player at Number One was ahead by more than any of the others. As for the remainder, they were all losing, with the bearded man probably running it pretty close with the stout sporting peer at Number Six.

This was the position when they took a recess, and the croupier at once rose to serve refreshments. The host also rose to assist him, while the guests leant back and talked among themselves of the play.

The studio, big though it was, was almost choked with the smoke from the scores of cigars and cigarettes which had been smoked during the play, and the Black Eagle walked across to a cord in the wall which worked one skylight in the front wall. He opened this wide; then he crossed to the other side of the room to a window which opened into the garden and drew that sash wide.

As he passed the buffet where his brother was employed with the silver dishes of sandwiches, he spoke to him in a low tone, telling him to go upstairs as soon as he had the chance and see if "Jacko" had returned.

He himself arranged the pails of champagne, and the hunchback slipped away. The Black Eagle had poured out nine glasses of the sparkling wine by the time the hunchback returned, and as he paused close to him he shook his head, which meant that "Jacko" had not returned.

The Black Eagle gave no sign, but inwardly he was deeply puzzled. He was thinking over the matter the while he took care to place himself well between one of the glasses and the company at the table, and then, while he stood thus, the hunchback thrust out his hand. In it he had palmed a small phial, in the mouth of which had been thrust a small rubber dropper.

For the space of a couple of seconds or so his hand hovered over the wine-glass which the Black Eagle had indicated, and in that time a single amber-coloured drop of liquid fell into the bubbling wine. It dispersed almost immediately, leaving no trace of colour, and the Black Eagle did not need to taste the wine to know that it had left no taste either.

Then, while his brother held a silver tray, he placed the glasses on it one by one, and together the pair moved across to the table.

The Black Eagle courteously handed a glass to each of his guests, and the one which went to the bearded man at Number Five was the one in which the drop of amber liquid had fallen. Half an hour or so was consumed in partaking of the repast, then the play recommenced, and was again in full swing when things were brought to a dramatic end without the slightest warning.

At the time, the player at Number Nine (who was the host) was holding the "shoe," and had already made four turns on a two hundred pound bank against the bearded player at Number Five. This meant that the latter was then losing exactly three thousand pounds, and the Black Eagle did not pass the "shoe."

Instead, he waited for the other to buck the bank again, and the latter had just produced a further bundle of notes in order to do so when, as he glanced up to hand them over, his eyes seemed to remain fixed on the open sash of the window which gave on to the garden.

For the space of perhaps ten full seconds he sat rigid, his eyes showing hard and glassy through the slits of his mask. Then the whole company was startled by a hoarse, high-pitched scream as the bearded man pushed back his chair and staggered to his feet.

At the same instant there was a clatter and a whirring sound by the window, and, with his gaze already fixed in that direction, Sexton Blake saw a flash of brilliant pink and intense indigo as something swept through the opening and made straight for the man who had given the cry.

Blake had just time to see that what had entered the studio was a gigantic South American macaw of a blend of colour he had never seen before, when it was above the table, screaming and shrieking in a terrible fury and making a murderous attack on the man at Number Five.

The great bird that had come so suddenly out of the night seemed to have gone berserk, while the man who was the object of its fury had lost all semblance of self-control. He had knocked over the chair, and now, with arms raised in an effort to protect himself was backing away, step by step, while the macaw was at him with terrible curved beak and claws and wings. It was an appalling spectacle, and even more so when, in his frenzy of terror and fear, the man began to shout and scream the most awful oaths that ever issued from human throat.

In that crisis, the whole shell of civilisation dropped away from him. He was like a jungle savage bereft of all control, crazed by some nameless fear, surrendered to some stark terror. Several of the company got to their feet after the first few moments of dumbfounded stupor, and among these was Blake.

By now the oaths had changed to crazed appeals for help, and Sexton Blake was one of the first to dash forward to the assistance of the man who had changed into that screaming, maundering thing in those brief seconds.

The Black Eagle was also running forward, but both were suddenly pulled up short as the giant macaw made one more terrific assault, and, in the awful frenzy of the fear-driven creature, they saw him turn and run blindly across the room with the devilish bird in pursuit.

It seemed to be laughing in a savage triumph, like some imprisoned devil, and, as the man crashed blindly into one of the sideboards, it struck again. This time it got home with beak and claws, and, as the man turned with a further awful medley of oaths and cries, they saw that the mask had been ripped from his face, while his cheek had been opened in a terrible gash.

And just then, before either Blake or the Black Eagle could reach the man, another figure rushed in front of them.

It was the hunchback, with a piece of drapery in his hands, which he had grabbed up from a chair by one of the easels. Disregarding the murderous claws and beak of the macaw, he threw the cloth over the bird, and in one sweep of the arm had brought it down under control.

Then, while they stood watching him, he uttered some sound which they could not understand, and the next moment had run out of the studio, slamming the door after him. Blake and the host caught the body of the bird's victim just as he slumped forward in a dead faint, and the rest of the company gathered round while they endeavoured to resuscitate him.

He came round while Blake was still dabbing at the wounds in his face with a damp handkerchief, and swallowed some wine which the host held to his lips. They then assisted him to his feet, and, after one glance at the others, he demanded hoarsely to be assisted out of the place.

Blake and the Black Eagle each took an arm and helped him to the lounge adjoining. As they reached it, the hunchback put in an appearance, and at sight of him the bearded man began to tremble.

"That bird," he cried hoarsely, "have you killed it? Where did it come from? How did it come here? It was the pink macaw! I tell you I know it was! You saw it, didn't you?" And he turned towards the masked Blake.

Blake nodded his head.

"It was not imagination," he replied. "It was certainly a pink macaw that came through the window. What have you done with it?" he added, addressing the hunchback.

"It is gone," answered the latter. "I took it away and threw it outside. It has gone back whence it came."

"Threw it out!" screamed the bearded man, starting forward. "Why did you not kill it? Did you not see the blood on it? I tell you there was blood on its beak and claws when it came through that window! How did it get here? Where did that devil in feathers come from? Fool! Fool! Why didn't you kill it?"

And so the man went on, raving in his fear while the host spoke a few words to the hunchback, telling him to get a taxi.

They got him into the cab a few minutes later, and Blake volunteered to accompany him. The Black Eagle may have wondered a little at the way in which this masked guest of his had taken the initiative in assisting him to look after his stricken guest, but he asked no questions and made no objection to Blake leaving with the other.

Blake went back to get his coat and hat, and to whisper to his friend that he was leaving. Then he said good-night to his host and passed through the lounge.

The hunchback was standing by the door waiting to let him out, and pulled it open as Blake approached. Blake gave him a good-night as he passed, and then, as he reached the threshold, he drew up sharply.

There was no sign of the taxi which had been standing outside a few moments before, and, as he cocked his head to listen, Blake could just make out the sound of a motor vehicle of some sort which seemed to be just passing out of the crescent. He turned and glanced through the slits of his mask at the misshapen creature who still stood inside the door.

"He seems to have decided to go home alone," he remarked. "It doesn't matter. And, as I have already said good-night to your master, I shall not go back in again. Good-night."

And with that he started off across the crescent on foot, not a little puzzled at the strange events of the evening. He would have been a good deal more intrigued if he had known of that single drop of amber which had been placed in the glass of wine, and if he had seen the pink macaw at that moment, for the bird was swinging on the perch inside its cage in the room above the studio chuckling evilly.

CHAPTER 6.   The Tragedy Down at the Docks.

THE unwritten etiquette of the thing had made it impossible for Sexton Blake to ask the identity of the man who had been attacked by the pink macaw while he was at the house in the crescent. But in view of the extraordinary occurrence that had taken place, he was more than a little curious to know a little more about the affair.

As soon as he turned the corner he removed his mask and thrust it into his pocket; then he lit a cigar and lengthened his stride, for he intended walking through to Baker Street.

As he went along he pondered on what he had seen and heard—mostly the latter. And little wonder. At one moment they had been a company of conventional gentlemen engaged in a quiet gamble. It would have been impossible to have got together nine persons more representative of their class, and such a thing as melodrama or tragedy had seemed, at the time, very far removed from that circle.

That was at one moment. At the next, a pink-and-indigo winged, screeching devil had hurtled out of the dreary night, and in an instant chaos had reigned.

From a quiet, conventionally-clad, restrained individual, the bearded man in seat No. 5 had changed into a screaming, terror-driven creature, from whom the veneer of civilisation had dropped like magic. In those brief seconds he had changed into a berserk thing of screaming hysteria and horrible mouthings.

Rarely, indeed, had Sexton Blake heard such appalling oaths as had been emitted by the man in his terror, and among them were many that told Blake, as nothing else could have done, that, whoever the man was, he had learned his curses in the lowest company adrift on the seven seas.

And while he did not know the man's name, there was yet something vaguely familiar about his face. He felt that somewhere, sometime in the past, he had seen him before, and with this fugitive recollection came the subconscious thought that, wherever it had been, he had had some cause to dislike him.

Of course, Blake had known before he went to the house that the host would be David Stone—the name by which he was known there. And, equally, he knew that David Stone was the Black Eagle. But he had no suspicion that the Black Eagle had been employed for some months as a clerk in a shipping office in the City. When he had first learned that day that a private baccarat game was being run at the house in the crescent, he was mildly curious. He wondered if Stone was amusing himself, or if, by chance, he had some deeper motive at the back of his mind.

During the first part of the play, when he saw that the Black Eagle took the "shoe" in turn just as did the other players, he realised that the game was certainly not being run for financial benefit for his own pocket, for there had been no "house percentage" of any sort taken from the different pots.

And, indeed, he would have been very much surprised had this been done, for he knew that the Black Eagle was independent financially, or, at least, should be, if he had not lost his money recently. He had seen not a single suspicious occurrence until the pink macaw had suddenly flashed through the window and made its murderous attack on the man at No. 5.

Where had the bird come from? That was what Blake was asking himself. Was it a stray macaw that had escaped from somewhere, and, seeing the lighted open window in the house in the crescent, had dived in, and, being of a vicious nature, attacked the first person who had attracted its attention?

Certainly, before the bird had attacked him, the man at No. 5 had risen from his chair with a cry as if he had seen the bird before, and had some reason to fear that it would attack him. Why was that? Blake knew that, of late, a singular habit had grown up in London of making pets of parrots, and he had seen several of these birds being carried about the streets and the parks.

But a macaw was a very different proposition. It was not the type of bird which one usually made a pet of. It was too uncertain of temper, and, with its big, powerful beak and murderous claws, could do a good deal of damage when angry. He had, of course, seen macaws at the Zoo, and it was always possible that the bird which had come through the window might be one that had escaped from there.

But somehow Blake did not think so. Moreover, there were the words which the bearded man had uttered in his terror. They were mostly incoherent, but here and there Blake had heard bits which made him positive the man had some reason to fear some macaw, and a pink macaw at that. Never before had he seen a macaw of such an odd blend of colour. He had seen crimson macaws, and even deep pink macaws, but never one of that pale blush pink, and he knew that they must be as rare as albinos.

Then, again, in the lounge the victim of the attack had spoken of blood on the macaw's beak. There was blood on its beak and claws after it had clawed him and gouged his cheek open; but, even before it attacked, at the moment when it had hovered flapping about his head before striking, Sexton Blake had noted its terrible beak, and he was prepared to wager any amount that there had been dark red blotches on the bird's beak when it had come into the room.

Were those blotches blood? And were they to what the bearded man had referred?

Then, again, why had the misshapen creature who acted as the Black Eagle's servant (but who, Blake shrewdly suspected, was his brother) taken the bird away? It was, of course, a natural and quick-witted thing to seize a cloth and throw it over the bird in order to control it. But why rush off with it, and then state that he had thrown it outside?

It would have been more natural to keep the bird a prisoner at least until the victim of its attack had stated what he wished done with it. But then, in this instance, allowance had to be made for the fact that the queer creature was evidently not quite normal, and what he had said he had done with the bird might well be just the action such a mind would spring to.

And, finally, why, when he had apparently accepted Blake's offer to accompany him home, had the victim of the attack gone off alone in the taxi while Blake was getting his hat and coat? There were a lot of puzzling features about the affair, and Blake determined that the following morning he would call up the friend whom he had accompanied there and ask him if he could tell him the name of the man at seat No. 5. And at that he left it.

He came to his own house just about this moment, and on entering the consulting-room, where a cheerful fire was burning, found his young assistant Tinker sunk in the depths of a big leather club-chair reading. He looked up as Blake came in and absently asked if he had had a good evening.

Instead of answering his question, Blake at once took him to task for sitting up so late, and without more ado bundled the lad off to bed. Then, when he had thrown aside his coat and hat, he poured himself a night-cap, and lighting a cigarette, appropriated the seat which Tinker had been occupying.

He finished his cigarette and whisky; then he rose, and crossing to one of the bookcases, opened the leaded glass door and ran his hand along a set of the "Encyclopaedia Britannica." He selected a volume covering the first section of words beginning with the letter "M," and reseating himself, turned the pages until he came to an article dealing with macaws.

He read this through to the end, and when he had finished returned the book to the case. Then he poured himself a final drink, lit a fresh cigarette, and while he paced up and down the room began thinking over what he had read. And just before he turned out the light to go along to his own room, he summed up the result of his thinking in the single phrase:

"Well, anyway, there is nothing there that says the macaw is a night-flying bird, and I never knew before that it was. There is more than one queer thing about that pink devil that was out for murder tonight." And at that he left it for the time being.

But if Blake thought that was to be the end of the strange incident he was mistaken, for quite early the following morning he had a visitor in the person of Inspector Thomas, of Scotland Yard, who came to ask Blake to accompany him to a place near the East India Docks in the East End of London, in order to see the victim of what it was thought was murder, and while he willingly agreed to do so, Blake did not dream for a single moment that his visit there was to start his mind thinking again of the pink macaw.

In fact, during the night he had almost banished the matter from his mind, and had retained so little interest by the morning that he had given up the idea of telephoning to the friend he had accompanied to the house in the crescent in order to ask if he knew the identity of the man who had sat at No. 5.

On the way to the East End in Blake's car, the Grey Panther, Detective-Inspector Thomas gave Blake a brief history of the new case in which he was interested.

"Looks like murder, and yet there is something queer about it," he grunted as he settled down into the front seat beside Blake who was driving. "Shall I give you the details as we go along, or is your mind too much occupied in driving?"

"Shoot!" rejoined Blake laconically. "This old 'bus can find its own way— almost."

"Well," proceeded the inspector, "at first it looked like the result of an ordinary scrap. The victim is the mate of a small tramp-steamer lying at the docks at Poplar. He was found early this morning lying on the wharf against the back of a warehouse, and he had been dead for some hours.

"The discovery was reported in the usual way, and when it came through to the Yard I thought I'd look into it. I drove through there, and, after viewing the body, made a few inquiries.

"It appears that the man left his ship to go ashore last evening about six o'clock. As far as I can gather, he spent most of his time between a couple of public-houses near the docks, and, evidently, was drinking freely. In fact, the captain of the tramp and the second-mate of the same hooker tell me that he was a very heavy drinker at all times.

"Well, he was bundled out of one of the pubs, pretty early in the evening for being drunk and quarrelsome, and some of his 'friends' tried to get him to go back to his ship. I found one of those fellows— mate of another ship lying close at hand— and he swears that he and his companions left the fellow at the gate of his own wharf a little after eight o'clock.

"I put the bird on the grill, and, after some time, I managed to get more out of him. He tried to stick to it that he had not seen the murdered man after that, but finally he broke down and said that he and one of his companions had really seen the drunken man right along the dock until he was almost opposite where his ship was lying.

"Then they left him, but before they reached the gate they heard him cry out as if in fear. He says they ran back and found the mate lying on the ground moaning and clawing at the air.

"One of them lit a match—he doesn't remember which it was— and as it flamed up they saw that the mate had a terrible gash in his throat from which the blood was oozing in a heavy stream. He says he knew the man was done for, and that nothing they could do would save him. And—they were frightened of being found beside him. He says—and swears to it—that he bent down and tried to do something to help the wounded man. He also states that, as he did so, the mate muttered something which he could not quite catch as his throat was so filled with blood he could not articulate distinctly.

"I asked him to try and think what it was the man had said, and he replied that all he could make out were two words which sounded like 'pink macaw.'"

At that moment the Grey Panther took a sudden swerve in towards the kerb, and Blake missed a collision by less than a couple of inches. He succeeded with a quick twist in bringing the car back into the road, however, and as he did so the inspector glanced at him curiously.

"Narrow shave, that," he grunted. "Never saw you drive so badly before."

"I was—thinking of something else," answered Blake coolly. "Sorry I interrupted you. Go ahead with your story."

"Where was I? Oh, yes! Well, that is all I could get out of the fellow. He protests most emphatically that he knows nothing more of the affair. I asked if he had seen anyone lurking about the dock, but he said he had seen or heard no one. I haven't got hold of the man who was with him, but I have sent for him, and I expect they will have him by the time we get there. I went aboard the tramp to question the captain, and, in conversation with him, I discovered that the dead man had been very unpopular with the crew, and that any one of them might take a crack at him if the chance came along.

"I fancy he was one of the old type of bucko mates, from what I can learn, and that sort always has plenty of enemies who will do them in. But I am puzzled as to how he was killed. It was no knife that slit his throat open. I am positive of that. Nor was it a bullet that did the trick. The wound is deep and long and jagged, and —well, Blake, it looks just as if some one with very powerful fingers and heavy sharp nails had simply clawed his jugular clean out of his neck.

"That is why I thought you might be interested in having a 'look see.' I fancy we will find the job was done by one of the two who were with him a few minutes before, or else by some one of the crew of the old tramp on which he was mate. However, we shall soon be there. The body is still lying in the back of the warehouse on the wharf waiting for the divisional surgeon to make his examination."

The inspector broke off there, and, as Blake asked no questions they finished the rest of the journey almost in silence. It was a usual thing for the inspector to take Blake along with him whenever he was on a case that appeared at all out of the ordinary, for, aside from the fact that he liked Blake immensely, and owed a very great deal to him, he was a very canny person was Detective-Inspector Thomas, and he had learned the value long ago of keeping his eyes and his ears open when Sexton Blake was on the job.

Lots of times the inspector professed to a degree of denseness and stupidity which was no part of his make-up just in order to get Blake started on a theory, but while that little game had worked in the years gone by it did not fool Blake now, and he had more than a little harmless fun at times in concocting a hypothesis for the benefit of the inspector, in which he had not the slightest shred of belief himself.

But little did Inspector Thomas dream, as Blake guided the Grey Panther along Aldgate, that two words he had uttered in the course of his relation had come as a considerable shock to Blake, and had been the sole reason for the extraordinary behaviour of the car.

Guided by occasional grunts from the inspector, Blake finally located the gates of the dock which was their objective. There was a constable on duty outside who saluted as they drove up, and announced to his superior that the divisional surgeon had arrived and was then making his examination—also that two constables were with him.

Near the gates a small crowd had collected, but the constable was keeping them at a distance, and at sight of the car and its occupants they drew back a little.

Blake left the Grey Panther in the care of the constable, and made his way after the inspector along the dock. There was only one vessel lying alongside at the time —the tramp, of which the dead man had been mate—and a motley assortment of the crew hung over the side gazing towards the closed door of the warehouse in which the body lay.

As Blake cast his eyes over them, he had to confess that not one of them showed any signs of sorrow over their ship's loss, but he knew that, while any one of them might look as if he were capable of doing the "job," the chances were the majority was composed of regular everyday sailormen, of whom no more honest or likeable class exists.

He had knocked about the world too much to share the inspector's somewhat narrow estimate of the average sailorman who is sometimes a little hilarious during shore leave, and thus creates an impression regarding his class which is quite wrong.

The inspector hammered on the sliding door of the warehouse, and a few moments later it was pushed back a couple of inches or so by a constable. On seeing the man from the Yard he drew it back still further, and the two visitors entered.

On a big wooden packing case at one end the body of the dead man had been placed, and the bit of canvas which had covered it was now drawn back to permit the divisional surgeon to make his examination. He glanced up as the inspector and Blake drew near, and then went on with his work while the other two watched him.

Blake's eyes were keenly taking in every detail. He had missed nothing of what the inspector had said coming along in the car, and as he watched the doctor at his probing he had to acknowledge to himself that what the inspector had said about the gash in the throat had been truly descriptive of it. No knife had ever made that wound. Of that Blake was as positive as the inspector.

A blunt instrument such as a coarse file or screw-driver might have done it, or again, as the inspector had said, a powerful, heavily-mailed finger might have torn the flesh open in just that way. That was the ordinary opinion one might form. But, on the other hand, there were those words the inspector had uttered as they drove along.

The man he had questioned had stated that, just before he died, the victim of the mysterious attack had tried to speak, had, indeed, succeeded in uttering a few words of which the other could make nothing. Two of those words, breaking through the crimson flood which was choking the man, had been retained in the mind of the listener. The 'pink macaw' he had said they had sounded like.

The pink macaw! It is little wonder that the Grey Panther had swerved from its course as Blake heard the words. They were the very last he would have expected to be uttered by Inspector Thomas that morning. And it was those words of which Blake was thinking as he watched the doctor at work—thinking of them acutely, intensely and giving only an abstract attention to what the physician was doing.

Those words, and the others which had been uttered by the bearded man in the lounge of the house in the crescent off the Edgware Road the night before. What was it he had said? Blood— blood on the beak of the strange bird that had hurtled upon him through the bleak night and had attacked him like a nameless fury. Blood on beak and blood on claws.

And Sexton Blake knew he had been right. It had been no vision of mind inflamed by stark terror. It had been fact— real, deadly real. What did it mean? What could it mean?

Here on this dingy wharf in the East End of London a man had been killed in the hours of mid-evening—killed in a mysterious way which none could explain— if the man who had already been questioned was speaking the truth. He and his companion had heard a cry just a few seconds after leaving the mate. They had seen no one else. He maintained that they had heard nothing but just that cry. They had hurried back, and by the light of a match had found their late companion bleeding to death from a terrible wound in the throat. Then his strange words.

There was the fact that he had a good many enemies among the crew on the ship of which he was mate. Had one of them slipped over the side, and, under cover of the darkness, gouged his throat open with some instrument from the engine-room? Had he then stolen back aboard before the other two men had time to come back?

If that was the answer to the riddle, then it was safe to assume that the instrument which had been used was no longer on board the ship, but was most likely at the bottom of the dock. If the engineer of the tramp was a careful man, and if he was the usual Scots type it was safe to assume that he would be, then it might be possible to discover if one of the tools from the engine-room was missing.

That was a channel of inquiry worth exploring. But Sexton Blake was beginning to think this murder was no common killing. Why should the dead man have uttered those strange words? What could have made him speak of a thing which in itself was as rare as a white cobra?

That—and the strange occurrence which Blake had witnessed the night before. He was as positive as ever that the macaw was not a night-flying bird. Then where had that pink macaw come from at something like two o'clock in the morning with crimson patches on its beak? Where was its home? Why had it been abroad during hours which were unnatural to it? What had it been doing during those hours? And why had it found its way to the house of the Black Eagle?

Those were the thoughts which were occupying Blake's mind as he stood by the packing-case watching the surgeon at his work. So engrossed was he in the puzzle which filled his mind, that he had taken little notice of the features of the victim of the killing. His eyes had been resting on the jagged wound in the throat, and, after the first glance, he had been gazing at it without seeing it.

But as the surgeon straightened up, his eyes went to the cold rigid features of the dead man, and for the second time that morning he received a shock. He knew those features.

Blake gave no sign of his discovery, but stood studying them with every faculty concentrated on what he was doing. He knew them. Where had he seen the man before? He knew his memory was not playing him tricks. He never forgot a face, and he knew as surely as he stood there that sometime, somewhere, he had seen that man with the life in him, walking about as other men. But where— where— where?

Slowly, he turned and walked the length of the almost empty warehouse, paying no heed to the conversation which was taking place between the inspector and the doctor. He was striving to catch hold of something out of the past to give him a start in the association of ideas which would read him the answer to his unspoken question.

That man—mate of the tramp which lay at the dock—he had taken note of her name as he came along, but it had told him nothing—some other place—some other ship—that low-browed countenance, sullen and brutal even in death—where?

Back, back, back along the years his mind went probing, seeking after the elusive end of the thread. To every port in the seven seas it went, to every case which had taken him down to the sea, among the haunts of sailormen he sought, and then, like a bolt from the blue, he caught a fleeting recollection, lost it, grasped it again, lost it once more, then, as a vivid tropical scene burst upon him he held it.

Suva in the Fijis, that was where it had been. And now he had the whole scene before him. A hot, smoky day in the low part of the town—a waterfront dive filled with sailormen—a fight—the flash of knives—a man writhing on the floor with his blood spilling fast—that was it, and the man who had driven the knife home was the same who now lay dead in that warehouse.

Bucko Breen, that was the man, and Blake remembered that at the time he had been second mate on Bully Blood's hooker which was lying at Suva at the time.

Bucko Breen, and Bully Blood, and then his knuckles grew suddenly white as his fingers closed spasmodically, for his mind had jumped straight from Suva to the house in the crescent off the Edgware Road.

Bully Blood! Why, the bearded man in his fashionable evening clothes and his aping of the manners of a sahib was none other than Bully Blood himself! Years it had been since Blake had seen him, but he was sure, sure that he was right.

Bully Blood! Good heavens! That explained the appalling oaths which had issued from between his purple lips when the veneer had dropped from him. Bully Blood! What was the man doing in that company? Did the Black Eagle know anything about him? Were they perchance running mates? Who had introduced him to the circle—one of the hardest in London to get into?

And here, in this dingy warehouse, lay a dead man who had been connected with the past of Bully Blood. Dead he lay, and died in a horrible fashion, as if spectral fingers had torn the throat from him. Bully Blood and Bucko Breen. One in the exclusive West End of the heart of the world; the other in the scuppers of the same great city. And, the coincidence, —if coincidence it was—of that pink devil in feathers. What did it mean?

Sexton Blake's eyes were a hard steely grey as he turned and walked back to the other end of the warehouse, and his nostrils were quivering on the impulse of the surface nerves for, like a seasoned hound, he had caught a scent, and he was straining at the leash to be away on the track of it—a breast-high scent which reeked of ships and the salt seas, of blood and the mephitic stench of waterfront dives, of the wild passions of men who know no law, and of a pink macaw, a pink and indigo devil in feathers with a crimson-stained beak which could so easily tear a man's throat to ribbons.

CHAPTER 7. Sexton Blake Makes Some Astonishing Discoveries.

SEXTON BLAKE rejoined the inspector and the surgeon just in time to hear the last bit of their conversation, and that was sufficient to tell him that they both shared the opinion that the murder had been done with some blunt instrument such as the type of wound would suggest. Blake waited until they had finished, then he said to the inspector:

"Did you mention to Dr. Graham what the murdered man was supposed to have uttered while he was bleeding to death?"

"No, I hadn't," answered the inspector. "I don't attach any importance to it."

"What was that?" asked the physician.

"The inspector says that during his cross-examination of one of the men who was with the victim a few moments before he met his death, the man told him the stricken one tried to say something, but all he could catch of it was a couple of words or so."

"What were the words?"

"The inspector says the man tells him they sounded like 'pink macaw.'"

The doctor shrugged. "His imagination," he said curtly. "The poor fellow was probably trying to say something—I don't question that, but the other was probably muddled or drunk in thinking those words. I don't think we need attach any importance to that."

"Probably not," said Blake mildly. Then to the inspector: "I suppose you will make further inquiries on the ship."

"Just how do you mean?" asked Inspector Thomas.

"Well," said Blake, "both you and the doctor seem to think the killing was done with some sort of blunt instrument. I have no desire to cast suspicion on anyone on board the tramp, but I think you told me the captain had intimated that nearly every man-jack of the crew hated the mate, and a blunt instrument, such as you think, may have been used, might have come from the engine-room. It might be a good idea to catechise the engineer and have him search among his equipment to see if a tool is missing. If it was done by someone on the ship, and a tool is found to be missing, then it might be located in the mud at the bottom of the dock. That is just a suggestion of mine. You may have thought of something else."

"No, that had already occurred to me," said the inspector unblushingly. "I intended having another talk with the captain, and also I want to investigate the crew. Will you come along with me?"

"I should like nothing better," responded Blake; and a few minutes later, when the divisional-surgeon had taken his departure, they crossed the gangway to the deck of the tramp. They found the captain below, and there the inspector put a string of questions to him while Blake listened and studied the hard-bitten countenance of the man.

The captain had no objection to the engineer being questioned, and when the inspector had finished with him, sent for that officer to come along. The engineer proved to be a Scotsman, just as Blake had thought might be the case, and he was highly indignant at the suggestion that any of his engine-room tools might be missing.

However, under the authoritative demand of Inspector Thomas, he could not refuse to take an inventory, and shortly went off, grumbling to do so. Then, with a glance at Blake, the inspector rose, with the remark that they would return when the inventory had been finished. Blake rose, too, but before he left the saloon, he turned to the captain and said, casually:

"By the way, captain, who are your owners?"

"The Gore Shipping Line," answered the other curtly, for he was in a bad temper from the grilling the inspector had been giving him.

"I don't think I know them," remarked Blake in the same casual tone. And with that he followed the inspector on deck.

They crossed to the wharf and made their way to the gates. Just as they reached the road, a constable came along with a message for the inspector stating that the second man who had been in the company of the dead man a few minutes before he met his death had been located, and was then at the police station. As they were already bound for there, the inspector told the constable to get in at the back, and Blake drove the Grey Panther round to the station.

They found the man who had just been brought there to be a longshoreman who had been found at his work on some other docks, and a question elicited the fact that he had not been allowed to hold any conversation with his mate who was still in one of the cells.

Then the inspector put him on the grill, and at first the man denied that he had seen the dead man after they had left him at the gates. But when he was told that his mate had already acknowledged that they had gone on to the wharf, he gave in and related almost word for word the same story that his companion had told. If it wasn't true, then, Blake concluded, the pair of them had fixed up the story the night before, and had agreed to tell it and stick to it if they were questioned.

There was one thing, however, which he could not tell them, and that was what the dead man had said just before he died, for, unlike his companion, he had not bent over to hear what was said. When the inspector had finished with him, Blake asked if he could see the man's mate, and a constable took him and the inspector along to the cell.

When the man approached the door, protesting loudly against being locked up, he was silenced sharply by the inspector, then Blake put his head to the grating and said:

"Look here, my man, if you are innocent you will have nothing to fear. If you have told the truth, then you will soon be released. The inspector here will tell you the same. But there is one thing I should like to know, if you wish to tell me. You have already been warned that anything you may say will be taken down in writing and may be used against you, but you have already volunteered a statement, and it is on one part of that I should like to ask you a question."

"What is it?" growled the man, suspiciously.

"You said in your statement that the man who was found dead last night tried to speak just before he died."

"Yus—I said that. Wot abaht it, guv'nor?"

"Just this," said Blake. "You said that the words sounded like 'pink macaw.' Is that right?"

"A us— 'blinking pink macaw' wos wot he sed."

"Are you quite sure of that?"

"In course I am! Wot y'er think—that I'd make it up? 'Ow could I think of such crazy words as them, I arsks yer?"

"I believe you," said Blake cheerfully. "And I'd cheer up if I were you. I don't think it will be long before you are free."

With that he turned away, and the inspector, who had been frowning during the conversation, followed him. But it was not until they were back in the Grey Panther that he voiced what was in his mind.

"What was the idea of that question?" he asked when Blake had started the car back towards the wharf. "I mean about those words.

And why did you tell him you thought he would soon be free?" he went on suspiciously. "That pair of birds might have done the job, Blake."

"Entirely possible," responded Blake with a faint smile. "As for the question— well, my dear inspector, wasn't it natural to see if he would repeat the same words? They are not common words, and if he had made them up on the spur of the moment while he was making his statement to you, why, he might have forgotten them the second time he was questioned, or put them differently. It didn't do any harm to test him on them."

The inspector grunted, but he was not entirely satisfied with Blake's explanation, he had had experience in the past of the extraordinary way in which the great criminologist's mind functioned, and he never could be quite sure when Blake was mildly pulling his leg and when he was serious.

On arriving back at the dock, they made their way at once on board the tramp, but on that line drew a blank. The engineer was quite positive that every one of the engine-room tools was in its proper place, and leered in sardonic satisfaction as he gave the information to the inspector. There was nothing more to be done there at the moment, although Blake knew, from what the inspector said, that he still held the crew under suspicion, and that he would extend his investigations in that direction before the tramp would be allowed to leave port.

On the way up the dock, Blake asked him, in the same casual tone he had adopted all the morning, what was the name of the dead mate, and he was not surprised when the inspector told him it was "Breen." So his memory had not tricked him, he reflected, as he once more took the wheel of the Grey Panther to drive back west.

Blake dropped the inspector at Scotland Yard, and then drove on to Baker Street, where he found Tinker at work on the morning mail. In response to the lad's questions, he gave him a brief resume of the case at the docks, then he seated himself at his desk, and, drawing the telephone towards him, called up the gentleman whom he had accompanied to the house in the crescent the night before. When he had got through to him, he said:

"I realise that it is a little out of order to ask the names of any persons who were present at a certain place last night, but I have a particular reason for wanting to know the identity of one of them. But, first, perhaps you will tell me what happened after I left."

"Why, certainly, Blake!" was the response. "We broke up almost immediately after. I wasn't keen on playing any longer after that extraordinary occurrence. Nor were the others. We all left soon, and, incidentally, I cashed in your chips which you left on the table. I will send a cheque along to you during the day."

"I am extremely obliged to you. And now, can you tell me the name of the man who was—or perhaps I had better just say the one at No. 5?"

"I know whom you mean. I had no idea it was he until his mask fell off. His name is Gore—Barnfield Gore—and he is the head of the Gore Shipping Line."

And that was the third shock Sexton Blake got that morning.

He thanked the other, and after a few more words hung up the receiver. Then he took down a recent reference book and looked up the Gore Shipping Line. He read this in detail, after which he consulted a directory, finding that Barnfield Gore, Esq., lived at an address in Upper Brook Street. That done, he settled down to work, and was still so engaged when Mrs. Bardell came to announce that lunch was served.

After lunch, Blake informed Tinker that he was going out for a short time, but instead of sending the lad round to the garage at the back for the Grey Panther, he went himself.

From Baker Street he drove through to Upper Brook Street, and drew up in front of the number which the directory had given as the address of Barnfield Gore. He pressed the bell, and when a manservant opened the door, he inquired politely if his master was at home.

"He is at home, sir," answered the man, "'but he can't be seen. My master was taken suddenly ill during the night and his doctor has given orders that he is to see no one for the present."

"I am extremely sorry to hear that," returned Blake. "I trust his illness is not of a dangerous nature."

"Serious, but I don't know whether it is dangerous," replied the man. "If you care to leave your card, or a message, sir, I will put it with other matters to wait until he is better. Or if it is business, then you had better see his managing clerk, Mr. Burr, who is with the master now, but who could see you at the offices."

"No, thank you. I shall wait until your master is better," answered

Blake, and with that descended the steps.

As he drove away, his mind was again busy with this strange affair, and things were made no clearer by this sudden illness which had overtaken Barnfield Gore. Illness it was said—was it the result of the shock he had received the previous night, was what Blake was asking himself.

But of one thing he was now quite certain, and that was that the notorious "Bully Blood" and Barnfield Gore were one and the same person. Nor was that all. "Bucko Breen," who had been killed so mysteriously the night before, had been mate of a tramp which was owned by Bully Blood alias Barnfield Gore, and years ago Bucko Breen had been second mate on Blood's own hooker.

Blood had risen in the world—that was evident, but he hadn't gone so high that the same mysterious thing should not connect him with the killing of Bucko Breen, and that thing was the pink macaw.

What did it all mean? What could it mean? Sexton Blake knew that the pink macaw could reveal the secret if it could speak with a reasoning mind, but now that he had plunged into the mystery he was determined to ferret out the truth, for he had a hunch that deep down in the affair lurked the sinister being whom he knew as the Black Eagle, though what devilry he might be up to he could not guess.

That was his determination as he drove back to Baker Street that afternoon in late October, but he little guessed then how much water was still to run under the bridges of the murky Thames, and how much blood must still be spilled before he should pierce the veil which clouded his mental vision.

*   *   *   *   *

That evening, just as he and Tinker were sitting down to dinner, Sexton Blake received an urgent telegram from Paris which he could not ignore. The following morning he and Tinker took the Continental train from Victoria, and for the time being he had no option but to put aside the mystery which had been intriguing him so deeply for the past thirty-six hours.

And in the days that followed, the whole business was completely swept from his mind, for, on reaching Paris, he found himself and Tinker plunged into a major case which needed every atom of his concentration. But he was to have the other affair recalled to him very forcibly, and in an entirely unexpected way, very shortly after his return to London.

THE END OF PART ONE.

PART TWO.

CHAPTER 1.   The Master Hand—The Black Eagle's Power of Attorney.

LATE one afternoon in mid-November, David Burr, confidential clerk to Barnfield Gore, sat at the big desk usually occupied by his employer, at work on a thick bundle of shipping accounts. It was just about three weeks since the private baccarat party at the house in the crescent off the Edgware Road, and ever since that night Barnfield Gore had been absent from his office.

On his arrival home he had taken at once to his bed, and at the time he himself had thought that his indisposition was due to the shock of what had happened to him that night.

But the following day he had become considerably alarmed at his condition, and had called in a doctor, who had seemed somewhat puzzled over the case. Although his pulse had appeared quite normal, it was weak, and his temperature was persistently sub-normal. He had told the physician that he had suffered a shock, without going into details, and at first the medico had accepted this as the explanation of his condition.

But as the days went by and his patient grew worse instead of better, with an apparent paralysis setting in in the lower limbs and slowly but surely creeping upwards towards the trunk, the doctor had called in a well-known specialist in consultation.

This gentleman, however, seemed as little able to diagnose the exact trouble as his colleague, and, while different forms of treatment were applied and the patient kept under the constant care of experienced male nurses, the strange malady persisted in its course.

Certain phases of the trouble seemed to fit various diagnoses, but on any complete test for any one known disease it invariably broke down.

A second specialist who was called in had been as little able to define it as the other two, and, as his brain had not yet become affected, it did not take very long for a man of the intelligence which Barnfield Gore possessed to realise that he was a very sick man.

And with that realisation there crept into the mind of the one-time Bully Blood the cold fear of death. During this time he had been completely dependent on his confidential clerk, David Burr, to attend to all his business matters. On the very first day when the doctor who was first called in had told him that he would, of necessity, be

70

confined to his bed for some days at least, and that, under no circumstances was he to occupy his mind with business matters, he had found it necessary to give to his clerk, David Burr, complete general power of attorney which authorised the said David Burr to act for and on behalf of his employer in the same way and in every way which Barnfield Gore would have acted.

This power of attorney was so comprehensive that it practically made David Burr the Gore Shipping Line, and as such he had complete control of the finances of the line. Which was one of the things for which David Burr had been scheming.

Like a good and faithful servant he had called at the house in Upper Brook Street each evening after the close of business, there to report briefly to his sick employer how things were progressing.

As the days passed and his illness became more marked, and the symptoms of limb paralysis grew more definite, Gore was thankful that he had a clerk such as Burr to attend to matters for him.

But he would have felt very different about that if he had guessed for a single moment just how the fertile mind of his confidential clerk was employing itself.

In those three weeks David Burr had made considerable progress with the scheme he had hatched months before. One of his first acts on being placed in possession of Gore's keys was to make a thorough examination of his employer's private despatch cases, and, among the many documents he had the pleasure of perusing, he found, among other things, confirmation of certain suspicions which had been in his mind for some weeks.

That confirmation was essential to the success of his plans, and once he was possessed of that he knew that all he then had to do was to sit tight and wait until what he expected would happen did happen.

And he was not disappointed, for, on the afternoon referred to, while he sat checking over the bundle of accounts, a clerk from the outer office entered to announce that Captain Pindar, late of the sailing ship Corsair of the Gore Line, which had been wrecked about two weeks before in the Gulf of St. Lawrence, wished to see him.

David Burr nodded without looking up, and a few moments later his visitor was ushered in.

He was a tall, thin man with the hatchet face of a down east Yankee, and the minute he opened his mouth to speak one knew that Captain Pindar's cut did not belie his origin, for he talked in the deep, nasal twang which one hears the whole way from Boston to Calais, Maine.

He and Burr had seen each other on several occasions when the captain was in London port, and while Burr had taken careful note of the captain, the latter had scarcely noticed Burr, looking upon him with the usual skipper's contempt for the shore-bound office clerk.

But before his interview that afternoon was over he was to switch a good deal of attention to the temporary manager of the firm, and in a way that he little dreamed of at the moment he came in. He nodded in a curt way to Burr, and, without invitation, seated himself in the chair beside the desk.

After the first upward glance Burr went on with his adding until he finished the column of figures on which he was engaged; then he jotted down the sum on a paper block, and, laying the pencil down, raised his eyes and looked fully at his visitor. And in that moment Captain Pindar realised with something of a shock that the confidential clerk was by no means the nondescript individual he had previously taken him for.

"Well, Captain Pindar," said Burr pleasantly, "what can I do for you? I suppose you have just reached London."

"Yes," was the reply. "I got in from Liverpool this afternoon—cross from Quebec in the Andania. What's this I hear about the boss?"

"You mean Mr. Gore. I am sorry to say he is ill, a very sick man, captain."

"'Urnph! That makes things awkward. I had some important business to discuss with him. How soon do you think he will be about again?"

"It is impossible to say. He shows no signs of getting better, and for the time being, at least, his doctor will not permit him to have anything to do with business. And it looks as if you would have to possess your soul in patience, Captain Pindar, unless you wish to tell me your business. At present I am acting in everything for Mr. Gore. He has given me a complete power of attorney, but if your business is to see about getting another ship, then I am afraid it will have to wait. You see, captain, things in the shipping business are bad, very bad indeed, and instead of adding to his fleet, it is, I believe, Mr. Gore's wish to cut down his commitments as much as possible. The loss of the Corsair was unfortunate in a way, but at the same time she was well insured, and the firm rather stands to make a handsome profit than otherwise."

The seaman snorted.

"I tell you I have got to see Mr. Gore," he said harshly. "My business with him is of the greatest importance, and when he knows I am in London he will see me quick enough."

"I think not," returned Burr evenly. "And I have already said, Captain Pindar, that all business with the Gore Shipping Line must be transacted through me for the present. If your business with Mr. Gore is of a private nature—well, you may try to see him if you wish, but you will find it impossible. I suggest that you tell me what it is. I may be able to deal with it."

"You!" sneered the skipper, with another snort. "You!" he repeated. "I don't deal with lackeys. My business is with Gore, and Gore I will see, or—"

"Or it will be the worse for him. Is that what you were going to say, Captain Pindar?"

The other stared at Burr open-mouthed for a few seconds, then his lean jaws snapped to open again as he rasped:

"What do you mean, you blinking counter-hopper?"

David Burr rose and walked very leisurely across the thickly carpeted office to the door leading to the big outer general room. He turned the key in the lock; then, with the same absence of haste, he returned to his chair. Once again he faced the captain, this time with an odd smile on his lips.

"What do I mean?" he repeated, taking up the question. "I will tell you what I mean, my good swashbuckler. Listen to me. Before the Corsair sailed from Liverpool on her last voyage to Canada, you and Mr. Gore had a conversation. Things were already beginning to look bad in the shipping business, and I don't mind telling you, captain, that a good deal of Mr. Gore's ideas on that subject were due to remarks I made in his presence, written articles which I took care he should read, and other articles in various shipping journals which I myself wrote.

"Hold on—don't get excited—you will have plenty of time for that when I have finished. But right here I will tell you that it would have been of considerable benefit to you if you had taken a little more trouble in the past to study the man in these offices to whom you have just now referred as a counter-hopper. Before I finish with you, you cheap fish, I may tell you who I really am. Now listen.

"I said that you and Mr. Gore—or Bully Blood if you prefer it that way—had had a conversation here before you took the Corsair on her last voyage. You talked of many things on that occasion, Captain Pindar, and they were not altogether of 'cabbages and kings.' The principal topic, if I may say so, was the good ship Corsair.

"Now, I am not a shipmaster, captain, but I have sailed the Seven Seas in my time, and I have some slight knowledge of a particularly narrow and difficult passage through a certain point off the north-west part of Prince Edward Island, which juts well out into the Gulf of St. Lawrence. I can find plenty of old masters who do not know of the existence of that passage, for it is not every chart that shows it.

"But Bully Gore knew it, Captain Pindar, and so did you. And one thing that was settled on the day to which I have referred was that you were to take the Corsair through that passage on your outward voyage—or, at least, you were to take her part way through. Then, my dear swashbuckler, you were to lose her—lose your ship, captain, and when the job was done, and the insurance money received—a hundred and fifty thousand pounds, captain— you were to receive the sum of ten thousand pounds.

"You did your part of the job, captain, and now you have arrived in London to receive your blood-money—blood-money it is, for a good and honest ship has a soul, captain. But you are not going to touch a single penny of that blood-money. Even if you succeed in seeing Gore you won't get the money, for all Gore's affairs are in my hands, and I intend keeping them there. The hundred and fifty thousand pounds have been received from the underwriters—in fact, the cheque in settlement came in only to-day. But you won't see any of it, captain, and the joke of it is you daren't squeal, dare you? Now, what are you going to do about it?" And with that the confidential clerk leant back in his chair and regarded the seaman.

Whether what Burr had said was or was not true it would have been impossible to have told from the captain's face while he was speaking, for, after he had begun, the lean, hatchet face had been completely inscrutable. But that was only because he was holding down the terrific inward storm that was gathering by sheer will power until he should get the whole of it.

And no sooner had Burr finished than the other was on his feet, snarling and mouthing a stream of curses that would have done "discredit" to Bully Blood himself.

But Burr altered his calm attitude not a whit. His eyes were still humorous, and although his body was slack his hands were on his knees. The fingers curled in towards the palm in a curious way. He looked to be quite defenceless there in the low, swivel desk-chair, and Pindar seemed to think that it was he who controlled the situation. He was due for a severe enlightenment.

When he had quite exhausted his repertory of curses he came down to intelligible phrases, and for the better part of ten minutes he whipped Burr with the most scathing words he could muster.

Then, as his passion cooled a little under the violence of its own draught, so to say, he pressed his doubled fists on the edge of the polished mahogany until the red, mottled knuckles showed white, and his voice was deadly enough as he said:

"Know all about my conversation with Gore, do you! So Gore and I had a compact for the wrecking of the Corsair, did we? Quite a smart fellow, aren't you. And supposin' we did—what, has that to do with you? You're Gore's trusted man, aren't you! Going to double-cross the man who gives you your bread-and-butter, eh? You confounded guttersnipe a horseback, for two pins I'd get my claws in your throat and throttle you here and now. Yes, I did have a conversation with Gore before I sailed. It is quite right that the Corsair was never to return, and that I was to be handed ten thousand pounds on the day I returned to London.

"So now, you infernal white-collared pimp, if, as you say, the cheque-book is in your control, then get it out and write me a cheque for that sum, or, as sure as my name is Hiram Pindar, I'll throttle you before I go to see Gore. And he will see me, don't fear, and, what's more, he'll soon find means of settling you. The man doesn't live who got the better of Bully Blood and got away with it."

"You are mistaken," said Burr softly. "I have got the better of Blood more than once, captain, and I sit here while he lies in bed with half his body paralysed. And do you know why, captain? I will tell you— it is because I put him there, and he will stay just as long as it is my will. You fool, are you so blind that you think you have been dealing with a callow clerk whom you could back down with your oaths and threats?"

Like lightning the Black Eagle came out of his chair, and Pindar had a chance then to size up the magnificent physique of the man.

"Do I look like that! Do I talk like that? Listen, you poor fish from New England. Have you ever sailed along the Spanish Main and round the bend of South America past Devil's Island? Of course I you have. And you know what Devil's Island is. You know what type of man is hurled into the hell-hole, and what devils are set to guard him. Well, look at me well, for you are looking at one who spent twenty years in that pit of horror—twenty years, do you hear, and then got away from it.

"You think I became Bully Blood's clerk from necessity, do you? Why, you cheap swashbuckler, I could buy up Blood and all his ships and then not miss it from my wealth! And if it was not necessity that made me Blood's clerk, what was it? I will tell you.

"It was a vow of vengeance—a vow sworn in the sweating jungles of the Spanish Main just after I had escaped, from French Guiana. You say no man ever got the better of Bully Blood, and got away with it. You lie. I—I, the Black Eagle, have been getting the better of him for eighteen months, and to-day his affairs be at my mercy while he lies a paralysed and terrified lump in his bed."

"Have you ever heard of the Black Eagle. If you haven't go to Cayenne and ask. There are many there who can tell you much about him. And it is the Black Eagle who says that you do not touch one penny of the blood money from the Corsair you ship-murdering hound. Nor does Gore touch a penny. The cheque for that crime lies in my bank to my credit, and the money goes as I will. That is your answer. Now what do you propose to do about it? Do you still think you will gain anything by seeing Gore?"

Pindar's eyes had narrowed until they were mere wrinkled slits. He had drawn back from the desk, and his hands were hanging by his sides, his head was thrust forward aggressively.

"You're the Black Eagle!" he snarled. "Yes. I've heard of you. But you have made a mistake this time, my bucko. You may boast that you have got the better of Bully Blood, but you won't get the better of Hiram Pindar. I'm going to fix you, and it s going to be done right here and now. The Black Eagle, eh! All right, Mr. Escaped Convict, the French police will no doubt be quite glad to welcome you back, and the English police even more so to know that they have a criminal like you running loose in London. I'm going to fix you, and if you put up a yell all I have to say is that when I came in here I recognised you as what you are, and that you tried to attack me. I've handled lots of hot ones like you, and I am going to show you how it is done."

With that the skipper made a swift motion, and the next moment his hand came out from under his coat clutching a long-bladed knife, the steel of which glittered under the light over the desk.

If he expected the Black Eagle to show fear he was mistaken. Instead of doing so the man who had been so notorious among his fellows on Devil's Island drew to one side of the desk and laughed aloud— laughed as a man laughs in the sheer lust of blood and battle. His dark eyes were burning with an extraordinary light, and his shoulders were set in a way that any novice at the game should have been able to read.

But the man facing him had no streak of fear in him, no matter what a crooked maze his mind might be, and it was only too plain that he had recognised in Gore's confidential clerk the notorious escaped convict who was known as the Black Eagle.

If he could kill him—and he certainly intended doing so if he could—it would be easy enough to say that he had been attacked and had simply defended himself.

But Pindar was in ignorance of quite a few things, one of which was that the French Government would never trouble the Black Eagle while he stayed off French soil, and the other was the manner in which the convict had got his nickname of Black Eagle.

Nor had he ever seen those great hands tear three packs of playing-cards in half as easily as the ordinary man would have ripped half a dozen sheets of writing-paper to shreds—as Sexton Blake had once seen him do in the secret gambling club in Dover Street.

And even if he had, it would not have deterred him now. With that vicious length of steel in his hand he felt himself in a decidedly superior position, and while the Black Eagle still laughed the skipper sprang. He was round the desk in a couple of jumps, and with an oath lunged forward, driving the point of the blade with all his strength in an upward sweep towards the Black Eagle's throat.

It seemed as if the point would certainly reach its mark, for it was on the very touch of the flesh when the Black Eagle shot his head to one side, and with a twisting motion that was baffling in its speed he was in under the knife arm and up with both hands on the captain's throat.

Those hands—literally as terrible as claws of steel—tensed as they met the flesh, and the next second the captain had lifted clean off the floor while the Black Eagle jerked his head first to the left then to the right.

Choked though he was the captain gave vent to a groan which was jerked from under the heart in the agony of that throttling, and as the Black Eagle began to bend his head back and back and back the knife clattered dully to the carpet. Then the Black Eagle paused, and his deep eyes burned into the other's.

"Just like that," he whispered; "just like that—the sixteenth of an inch more to the right or the left, and the spinal column would have been snapped like a pipestem. That's the way I kill a man, captain, and that is the way I am going to kill you if you cross my path again. This time, and this time only, I am going to spare you for reasons of my own. But the next—look out, Captain Pindar, for I-will-do-it-just-like-this!"

And again he jerked the man's head to the left and the right until it seemed as if the column must crack. Then he loosened his hands, and, bending swiftly, picked up the knife. He tossed it contemptuously on the desk and pointed towards the door.

"Get out," he said curtly. Captain Hiram Pindar, picking up his hat in a dazed manner, staggered across the room without a word, unlocked and opened the door and passed out.

And as the door closed after him the Black Eagle reached for his cigarette-case, the while he laughed and laughed in a noiseless manner that was as sinister as the evil chuckle of the Pink Macaw.

CHAPTER 2.   The Black Eagle Explains the Situation.

FOR some time after the departure of Captain Pindar the Black Eagle walked up and down the private room smoking and thinking. A clerk appeared from time to time to ask about some matter of business, which the Black Eagle disposed of in the curt, crisp manner that the other employees had known from the first day he had entered Barnfield Gore's service. They, at least, had no illusions as to the driving force and cold domination of the confidential man.

Then, abruptly, he re-sealed himself at the desk, and quickly completed the task on which he had been employed when Captain Pindar had been shown in.

It was now past five o'clock, and when he knew that most of the clerks in the outer office must be gone, he too prepared to take his departure.

As on other evenings, it was his intention to pay a visit to the head of the firm, but he had made up his mind that the interview would be very different on this occasion; for the Black Eagle was at the point where he could pull his last string, and snatch the victory which he had planned so carefully for months past.

The outer office was empty when he passed through, and he descended in the lift to the street in the usual way. Since taking over control of the offices, it had been his custom to take a taxi to Upper Brook Street, and this evening he followed that course.

When the cab drew up in front of Gore's house, he paid off the man and mounted the steps. A young footman opened the door and greeted him with every sign of respect. As he took Burr's coat and hat, the latter said:

"Did a man giving his name as Captain Pindar call to try and see Mr. Gore, Burrows?"

"Yes, sir," answered the footman. "He came about an hour ago, and I must say, sir, he was very determined. But I had my orders, and I did not let him in."

"Quite right, Burrows," said the Black Eagle. "He called at the office—he would not discuss his business with me. I was going to warn you by telephone not to admit him if he called, but I knew you would act on your orders. How is Mr. Gore to-night?"

"The nurse says not quite so well, sir. The doctor was here about five."

"Very well. I shall go up now."

With that, the Black Eagle began to mount the stairs, and, on reaching the top, turned to the right along the hall there. Seated beside a small serving table, just outside the big front bed-room, was the male nurse, whose turn it was to be on duty, and as the Black Eagle approached he got to his feet.

Their eyes met for a moment, and in that brief space of time the one seemed to ask a silent question which the other answered in the same way. Then for the benefit of the footman who might still be in the lower hall, the Black Eagle said:

"How is Mr. Gore to-day?"

"Not quite so well, sir," answered the nurse in a low but distinct tone. "The doctor came about five. The patient seems to be having considerable difficulty in breathing, and if that condition increases the doctor says he will administer oxygen.

"From now on the window is to be kept open so that he may get as much fresh air as possible."

And as he nodded his head the Black Eagle smiled, for he had been waiting for just that report, knowing that it must come after a certain period of the course of the poison which his brother had dropped into Gore's glass of wine on the night of the baccarat game, and— the man before him was one of his own hirelings.

He moved forward to enter the room, and, as he laid his fingers on the handle of the door, he murmured:

"Get the footman away from the lower hall on some errand. The patient may kick up a row this evening, and I don't want the servants to hear anything."

The man nodded and started to move towards the head of the stairs while the Black Eagle pushed the door open and entered the room. He closed the door softly, and with a quick motion turned the key.

Then he walked across towards the big bed where, beneath the heavily-shaded light, he could see the tangled and unkempt beard of the patient against the white of the sheets and pillows. The sick man turned lustreless eyes on him as he drew up a chair and seated himself close to the bed, then he whispered weakly:

"It is you, Burr. Is there anything important to-day?"

"That depends entirely on how you look at it," answered the Black Eagle in a tone which Gore had never heard him use before, and which caused him, sick though he was, to twist his head and regard his confidential clerk with a puzzled frown.

"What do you mean?" he whispered. "I don't understand you, Burr, and there is something queer about your tone—or voice."

"Not at all," rejoined his visitor. "It is just that I have never spoken naturally to you before." And before Gore could say anything in response, he went on:

"Pindar is back in London. He was in the office to-day. He is howling for his ten thousand pounds."

He made the announcement carelessly as if it were simply an unimportant item regarding office routine. So carelessly did he speak, in fact, the man in the bed seemed quite at a loss to fathom whether there was anything behind it or not. He lay perfectly still for a full minute, his eyes on the ceiling, trying to whip his sluggish mind into action, for away down inside him something was hammering at him, warning him to tread warily.

At last he turned his head, and saw the mocking expression in Burr's eyes. In that flash he read the truth, but even then he stalled, trying to get his feet on solid ground of some sort.

"You mean Captain Pindar of the Corsair?" he asked.

"Quite right, Blood," answered the Black Eagle. "Captain Hiram Pindar of the Corsair. As I have told you, he turned up at the office this afternoon and wanted *to* see you. I told him you were too ill to attend to business, and could not even receive him to settle the little matter of ten thousand pounds blood money for the wrecking of the Corsair."

The sick man made a supreme effort and lifted himself in the bed. His eyes rolled in the effort he made to bring his mind into action to meet this attack which had come upon him as a bolt from the blue. But not even yet did he have a grain of suspicion as to just what could be the purpose of this mocking fiend who sat by the bed—in every way the complete antithesis of the restricted and respectful confidential clerk who had visited him every evening since he had been ill.

He could not bring himself to believe that it was an actuality which must be grappled with. He told himself that the disease had suddenly reached his brain, and that the whole thing was a hallucination— that his clerk was not really there at all. But the Black Eagle gave him no chance just then to test it, for he went on in the same cold tone:

"Let me finish. As I was saying, Pindar wanted his blood money. It wasn't that we did not have it to give him, for the cheque for a hundred and fifty thousand pounds came in to-day from the insurance people. But I told him there was nothing for him to receive, and it pains me to inform you that the rascal tried to drive a knife into my throat. I was compelled to throw him out of the office, and I thought it probable he would come on here and try to see you.

"As a matter of fact he did come, but was not admitted, and I suppose by now he is sitting in some drinking place inflaming his mind against me and—you. It was a pretty little piece of business, that, wasn't it—Blood? You and Pindar fixed things very nicely to collect that blood-money from the wrecking of the Corsair. And it came at a nice time, too, when the ship wasn't worth a half of that sum on the present shipping market. Naughty—quite naughty it was, Blood, and, of course, I could not permit such a thing to happen.

"Now, don't excite yourself, my good fellow. I know you are ill, and know to a dot just what you are capable of standing. In fact, I know far more about your illness than any of the doctors who are attending you, as you will learn later.

"You are going to learn quite a lot this evening, Bully Blood, alias Barnfield Gore, so compose yourself to listen. It will explain quite a lot of puzzling things to you. Now then, I shall begin—where? Why, I think it had better be with the pink macaw.

"That makes you flinch, does it? I thought it would. But just listen, Blood, and you will find an answer to every question you are now asking yourself. You are racking your brains as to whom I can be. You are asking yourself what I have to do with Bully Blood and the pink macaw. You are telling yourself that this is all a figment of your imagination due to the disease which is creeping through your body.

"Maybe it is, Blood—maybe it is. Perhaps I am not sitting here at all. You may be in a delirium just picturing all this. Perhaps it is that, and perhaps it isn't. But— listen just the same.

"I said I would begin with the pink macaw. Just go back some years, to a time when you were skipper of your own old hooker—1 mean the old dingy black-and-red painted tub which you used to sail all over the seven seas. Remember one day in a certain bay in a little-known part of the Melanesians, do you recall the first time you saw the pink macaw? Do you remember how the bird took a wild hatred of you the moment it saw you? Do you know why? Did you ever wonder?

"I'll tell you what I think is the reason. I think it is because the bird held the spirit of some poor sailorman, whose life you had beaten and battered and kicked into eternity. That is what I think, Blood. But, whatever the reason, the bird hated you; and when you would have had it killed the sailorman who owned it, who had picked it up in South America, and who came aboard your ship after having been wrecked there, in the Solomons, refused to let you harm it. What did you do?

"You did just what you have done on more than that occasion. You had the man strung up to the fore-topmast, and you let the rolling vessel swing him back and forth in a merry devil's swing until he was battered to a pulp against the mast. Then you cut him down and threw him over the side. He didn't die—just then. Some natives took him ashore, and the bird went with him. But he died that night, and to another sailorman he gave the pink macaw.

"That sailorman was but a lad then, but he was to be a grown man before you again saw the pink macaw, Blood. And you, the bully of seven seas, were to have many a man-handling to your credit before you were to see either of them."

At that point the Black Eagle broke off, and, despite the doctor's orders, lighted a cigarette. Then he proceeded, but now his voice was extraordinarily softened as he said:

"I had a brother. We were children of the same mother. He was not made as other men were made. The good God had chosen to fashion him differently, but in compensation he gave him the nature of an angel and the voice, of a heavenly chord. I went abroad, and while I was on the Continent, my brother ran away to sea. I did not know anything of him for many years, for trouble came to me, and I was shut away from the world for twenty years. But during that time my brother, this poor misshapen bit of humanity who was as guileless as a child and as sweet-natured as an angel, fell into the hands of men like you, Blood. They made him more misshapen than Nature had made him. They marked him and broke him and flayed him. What was bent was twisted; what was twisted was broken. All those years when I, his natural guardian and protector, could not be with him, he was in the hands of hounds like you, Blood. And what did I see when

I found him! There is no need to tell you, for you know.

"He sailed under you once, Blood, but you did not mark him as badly as others. It was Bucko Breen who tore one of his ears almost from his head. That was just a bit of playfulness on Breen's part. And now I shall tell you what happened to Breen. You recall that one of your old iron tubs— the Tiber—was lying at the docks here, in London, a month ago. And you will remember, Blood, that one night, the night you were attacked by the pink macaw, you were gaming in a certain house in a crescent off the Edgware Road.

"You see, I know a lot, Blood. And, indeed, why shouldn't I, when it was I who lured you there. Months and months ago I spotted you in the 'Diamond Room' of a certain secret gambling club in Dover Street. I had been looking for you for a long time then. I will tell you why presently.

"When that club was temporarily closed, I knew enough about you and the circle you mixed with to have little difficulty in getting you included in the private game which I started at that house in the crescent. Yes, it was I who was your host there, Blood, though little did you think that the same man whose house showed every sign of wealth was also your modestly-paid confidential clerk, David Burr.

"I knew you were a rotten baccarat player, and that is why I arranged to get you into that game. It was just one part of my plan. I wanted you to lose heavily, and you did. I did not want your money for myself. I did not care who won it as long as you lost it. And it wasn't necessary to run a crooked game in order to achieve my end. You were a wild player and always 'rode your shoe' too long, and the man who does that must be a consistent loser, Blood.

"Do you know how much you lost in my house? I can tell you. Up to your last night there, you were totalling just a little under a hundred thousand pounds. Not the major fraction of your wealth, Blood, but it was enough as a start, and it was enough, too, to make you sell certain of your best securities. I, as your confidential clerk, knew when you were doing that. I was out for your blood—by which you were named.

"And your fear of the pink macaw was what I built on. That night—that night, when you were attacked, you were not mistaken, if it was real, in thinking there was blood on the beak and claws of the bird. You haven't been told that on that same evening Bucko Breen, the mate of the Tiber, died in mysterious circumstances. I kept that from you, Blood. But he died; and, just before he gasped his last, he was heard to choke out certain words.

"What do you think those words were, Blood? I will tell you. They were: 'The pink macaw.' And it was late, very late, that night when the pink macaw made its appearance in the studio of my house in the crescent with blood on its beak and blood on its talons. At the inquest they called it murder by some person or persons unknown, and the mystery is as great to-day as it was then, Blood. But you should have seen Bucko Breen's throat. I went to the inquest, and I saw. It was ripped open, dragging the jugular clean out, Blood, just as if the beak of a powerful bird had gouged it. And it was that night, I repeat, that the pink macaw appeared at my house and attacked you. Strange, isn't it, Blood?

"It wasn't the shock of that attack that laid you low. You didn't know, but I will tell you now that your wine, that night, was doctored with a powerful and slow-acting poison. It is that poison which is in your system, Blood. It is that poison which is stealing your life away. The doctors may well be puzzled. They have never seen it before, and, even if they could identify it, they could not name the antidote. It is I only who can produce that, and if it is my will that you should die, then die you must, and no human aid can save you.

"But first, Blood, you must suffer—to the limit. You haven't finished yet. You have a long score to pay, and I am the collector. For three weeks I have held your power of attorney. In that time I have had my will with your affairs. To-night you are a broken man, Blood.

"You do not possess a penny in the world. Every pound of your fortune has passed to me, and every one of your ships has been sold. Not wrecked, as you and Pindar destroyed the Corsair. On, no! I am too careful to make that mistake. And not only are you ruined financially, and helpless here under the poison which is taking your life drop by drop, but I have only to say one word and you are unmasked as a criminal as well—you and Pindar. I leave you to imagine what the insurance people would do if they knew the truth about the Corsair. And now, just a little more, Blood.

"Cast your mind back to one hot afternoon, some years ago, when you lay in your old hooker off the Spanish Main. That was the second occasion on which you saw the pink macaw. You didn't know it was the same bird, but it was, Blood, the same which caused that long scar under your ear. Do you remember what happened that day?

Do you remember the boy who came aboard with the bird and a companion? I was that companion, Blood. Do you recall how your bullies held me while the boy's life was hammered out against the fore-topmast in the same way you had broken the body of the other sailorman who owned the pink macaw?

"Do you recall how you tried again and again to kill the bird and failed—how, finally, I broke free and tore your own gun out of your hands, forcing you to have the boy lowered and set free? The boy died on the beach that night, Blood, and it was then he told me the other story about the pink macaw. I promised him I would avenge him, Blood, and that is why I sought you out— that, and to take toll of you for the things that you and your kind had done to my brother.

"I was on my way north then, but I could not move at great speed, for I had scores of my own to settle on the way. I was on Devil's Island for twenty years, Blood. I escaped from Cayenne, and, away up the Essequibo, I cleaned up a quick fortune in diamonds. That afternoon, off the Spanish Main, I had a letter of credit in my belt that you would have done more than murder to possess. If you have been at Cayenne or at Georgetown, you will have heard of me, Blood. Men on Devil's Island called me the Black Eagle, and it was a bad day for you when the Black Eagle swore a vendetta against you, Blood.

"That is what I had to say to you, Blood. A pretty tale, is it not? Now, you know what happened to Bucko Breen! You know, too, that Pindar has returned, and is on the warpath. And you, Blood, what of you? You are lying here, victim of a disease that none but one person can cure, and that person is I. You are broken financially, and you are a criminal for whom the insurance people would have no mercy. Captain Bully Blood—Captain Barnfield Gore! That is what the Black Eagle had done to you—the Black Eagle and the pink macaw, Blood. And does the pink macaw exist? Who knows? It may be all a dream of yours. I, too, may be unreal.

"You can think of that when I am gone this evening, Blood. Perhaps, after all, it is just your confidential clerk, David Burr, who is sitting here trying to make the day's report to you, and you can't understand it because you are delirious and have got the past mixed up with the present. Perhaps it is just the devils in your brain that are making you think I am saying all this. Perhaps it is the devil that dwells in the pink macaw, Blood.

"But if it is, or if it isn't, keep one thing in your sane understanding, Blood. In three days it will end. The Black Eagle will strike his last blow, and you will again see the vision of the pink macaw. Will there be another throat torn open, Blood— will there be another? Quien sabe!"

But there was no need to go past that point, for as he rose and bent over the bed the Black Eagle saw that his victim was unconscious. He stood looking down at him for a long time, his eyes filled with cold and deadly hatred, merciless and cruel.

Then he straightened up, and, as he crossed the room towards the door, he laughed and laughed again in that soundless, sinister way in which he had laughed in the office.

CHAPTER 3.   The Confession of Captain Bully Blood.

SEXTON BLAKE and his young assistant, Tinker, had been in Paris for the better part of three weeks, and on their return to London they naturally found a great many matters had piled up during their absence, some of which could be handled in the course of ordinary routine, but others which were of an urgent nature necessitating immediate attention.

Blake's clientele had grown to enormous proportions, and for a long time past he had been threatening to establish an additional secretary at Baker Street, and probably would have carried out his intention had it not been for an inherent dislike for changing the established order of things.

Besides, when they were in London, Tinker had no difficulty in keeping abreast of the routine that arose, and it was only when they were both off on a case that things got the better of the lad.

On this occasion there seemed to be a bigger bunch of stuff than usual to attend to, and within half an hour of their arrival at Baker Street the pair were at it as hard as they could go—Tinker taking down dictation as fast as Blake could shoot it at him.

It was while they were thus employed on the morning after their return that the housekeeper, Mrs. Bardell, came in to announce a visitor, and when she had ushered the caller in, Blake discovered it was a well-known Harley Street physician whom he knew personally quite well.

A professional man himself, the doctor was able to appreciate the signs of industry before him, and after the first few words of greeting he lost no time in coming to the point.

"I shall not take much of your time—can see you are rushed," he said as he accepted one of Blake's cigars. "Came to see you yesterday, but you had not returned from abroad—your housekeeper said you had telegraphed saying you would be back same night. Can you spare the time to give me the benefit of your advice?"

"It all depends, Dr. Green," answered Blake, waving Tinker away to his desk. "As you can see, I am up to the ears in work that has piled up during my absence, and I have already come across several things that will need my early attention. But let me hear what it is."

"It is connected with a patient of mine. His name is Barnfield Gore, and he is the head of a shipping line in the City. Know him?"

"Not personally, but I have heard of him, and I think I have seen him," answered Blake. "What is the trouble?"

"He has been ill for about three weeks. When I was first called in he told me he had been subjected to a shock, and it was on that basis I treated him—advised a few days' rest in bed, and so on. But before two days had passed I saw that there was something very much more than just nervous shock the matter with him, and, as I grew more and more puzzled, I called in another opinion. My colleague couldn't seem to diagnose the case any better than I, and still later I had a third opinion.

"There is no need to go into the case in detail now. If you wish I can let you have a full chart which will cover it from the beginning. It is sufficient to say that it appears to be a strange form of disease which is beginning to cause a form of paralysis beginning with the lower limbs and creeping upwards towards the trunk. The patient's pulse is steady enough, though very weak, but his temperature is persistently sub-normal, and, while his mind is clear, he is in a constant state of worry over business matters. This worry has become very greatly accentuated since the night before last, and it is on his own request that I have come to see you.

"There is undoubtedly something on his mind—something of a serious nature. Moreover, he has suddenly become convinced that he is going to die, and I don't know that he isn't right about that. Unless we can identify the strange malady which has attacked him, I do not see what can save him. But just now he keeps on asking that you should be sent for, and when I returned last night and told him that you were abroad I thought he was going to collapse entirely.

"I should take it as a personal favour if you would try and spare the time to see him. Unfortunately, I cannot tell you exactly what it is, because he refuses to confide in me. He is so secret about it that he has sworn me to keep his request from the knowledge even of his two male nurses. I have just left him, and he is still begging to see you. Could you manage to come?"

"It may be just some sick fancy," remarked Blake. "To tell you the truth, doctor, I am badly pushed just now with all these matters to attend to, but in a case of this sort I hardly feel like refusing. Is your car waiting?"

"Yes. If you will come along I can drop you there. It is not necessary for me to come in with you. I doubt, anyway, if he would allow anyone else in the room—even his physician."

"Very well, I shall come."

With that Blake rose and made his way along to his dressing-room, where he slipped into an overcoat and got his hat and stick. Then he rejoined the doctor in the consulting-room, and, after a few words to Tinker about the work on which the lad was engaged, he followed his visitor out to the street. Nor had he given the slightest sign to the medico that the identity of his patient and the illness which had attacked him held any more interest for him than would have been the case if he had never heard of Barnfield Gore, or—if he had not been present one night about three weeks before at a certain house off the Edgware Road.

Since that night and the following day, when he had gone to the East End of London with Inspector Thomas, of Scotland Yard, Blake had dropped his interest in those matters.

He had been too much engrossed in the case which he had been following on the Continent to give his mind to anything else, and, beyond a brief clipping of the inquest on the mate of the Tiber, which he had found enclosed in an envelope from the inspector on his return the previous evening, he had heard nothing more of the tragedy, nor of the affair at the house in the crescent off the Edgware Road.

Not that the matter had passed entirely from Blake's mind. It was filed away, so to speak, and, in the ordinary course of events, when he had time to revert to it, he would have had a talk with the inspector about the inquest, for he had been more than a little intrigued about what was said to have been Breen's last words.

That, following on the strange occurrence at David Stone's house, and the fact that Breen was employed on one of the ships owned by Barnfield Gore, had been sufficient of a coincidence to call up all his professional instinct. Nor was his interest lessened by the fact that he had recognised Breen as a bucko mate he had seen years before, and through that recognition had placed Gore as the notorious Bully Blood.

Therefore, even in the midst of the work which had piled up during his absence abroad, he was willing, for reasons of his own, to go along and find out why Barnfield Gore, whose condition seemed to have taken a serious turn since the night he had been attacked by the pink macaw, was so anxious to see him.

But as has been said, he made no mention of these matters to the doctor.

He was deposited by the latter in front of Gore's house in Upper Brook Street, and without his name being given, was conducted by the physician up to the first floor where Gore's bed-room was situated.

As he passed through the lower hall, Blake took note of the footman who admitted them, and also, on the upper floor, of the male day-nurse who was seated at the service table outside the door of the sick-room.

On entering the room, it needed only one glance for him to see that the doctor had by no means exaggerated when he said that Gore was a very sick man. He was a startling contrast to the man Blake had seen three weeks before. His face was pinched and drawn, and where it was free of the black straggling beard, was of an unhealthy looking yellow. His eyes were feverish and sunken.

One hand, which lay outside the coverlet, looked terribly thin and transparent, and he kept moving restlessly, almost continuously, as if something within him would not allow him to rest in peace.

Whatever Blake may have thought of the notorious Bully Blood, he could not help but feel a certain pity for this wreck of a man who lay before him. It was so different from the husky bucko skipper who had spread terror among sailormen on every sea. The doctor had closed the door after him, and when they were standing beside the bed made the introduction in a low tone. The sick man acknowledged it with a little movement of the head, and whispered something about being glad Blake had come.

Then the doctor took his departure after promising to see that the male nurse was given some duty which would keep him busy in the basement for some time; and when the door had closed after the physician, Gore made a gesture asking Blake to lock it. Blake did so and returned to the chair beside the bed; then he leant forward and, speaking in subdued tones, said:

"You sent for me, Mr. Gore. What is troubling you? And in what way do you wish my advice?"

Gore turned his head so he could look at Blake; then he said:

"I have much to say to you, Mr. Blake, and I beg that you will listen to me. I am a very ill man, and I know that I shall die soon. But before I do so I want to— confess certain things, and also to bring a certain man to book.—I—"

"Just a moment, Mr.Gore," put in Blake, laying one hand on the edge of the bed. "Before you begin, let me say something. Am I right in taking it that you have been ill ever since the night you received the shock of which Doctor Green has told me?"

"Yes."

"Do you think your illness is entirely due to that shock?"

"That is one of the things I want to tell you. I know now that it isn't. I have known since the night before last, but I have not told the doctor—yet. I wanted to see you first. I am the victim of a devil in human form."

"Then let me say something," went on Blake. "It may make it easier for you to get to the point. I may tell you that I was a guest one night, three weeks ago, at a certain house in a crescent off the Edgware Road when you were the victim of an extraordinary attack. As a matter of fact, it was I who offered to accompany you home, but when I went to get my hat and coat and returned you had gone off without me. I know, Mr. Gore, that you were, at one time, a well-known man on the high seas."

"You!" whispered Gore hoarsely. "You —Sexton Blake! Were you there that night?"

"I was—as I have said. It is part and parcel of my profession to be persona grata at such places, Mr. Gore."

"And you say you know how I was known years ago? You know that I was—"

"I know that you were known as Bully Blood," said Blake filling in the pause.

"And do you know the identity of the man who was the host that night of which you have spoken?"

"You mean David Stone? Yes—I know his real identity."

"Ah! You know that he is an escaped convict—that he was a convict on Devil's Island, the French penal settlement off the coast of South America. You will know then that he is a devil in human form. That is well, for it makes it easier to tell you; and I shall speak the truth. If you know that I was Bully Blood, you may think I will lie. But I shall speak the whole truth. I am a stricken man, and— and I cannot die until I have got all this off my mind."

He paused then, and Blake waited, thinking to himself: "The man is in a sheer funk. He is afraid of Death. He is a victim of remorse in an acute form. All right—if he wants to make a confession, I will listen to it. Out of it all some wrong may be righted—who knows."

And he waited patiently until Gore began again. He started soon then; and in broken sentences, breaking off at times to gather his strength for a renewal of the effort of forcing himself up in the bed in the excitement of the fear which was gripping him.

Bully Blood made a full confession to the grave-faced man who sat by his bed. And he told the truth. Of that Blake was certain as he listened. He spoke of things he needn't have spoken of. He accused himself of sins which only he himself could have known of. He ran the full gamut of twenty years on the high seas, and when he came down to the present Sexton Blake gave his keenest attention.

Gore told of how he had made money during the war, and, coming ashore, had started his own shipping line. He told how, for a time, things had prospered; but then how, as shipping values began to fall and he himself was losing large sums in gambling, he had found himself pinched for money, and had had to realise on large blocks of capital to keep things going. Then he confessed how he had made up his mind to over-insure his ships, and to have as many of them lost at sea as possible, thus retrieving his fortunes by the money he should receive from the marine underwriting companies.

Then he came to the night at the house in the crescent off the Edgware Road, and from that jumped abruptly to the visit of his confidential clerk, David Burr, which took place the night before Sexton Blake returned from Paris. As he related what had taken place that evening, a great many things began to take form in Blake's mind, but he was not even then prepared for the disclosure that David Burr was David Stone, although he knew David Stone was none other than the Black Eagle.

That part of it was little more than a repetition of what the Black Eagle had said to Blood that night. And then from that the sick man jumped back to the mysterious death of Bucko Breen, and this brought him to the pink macaw.

"I don't know whether that feathered devil was real or not," he moaned, by now quite exhausted from the medley of emotions he had just gone through. "That devil who came here said it might be or might not be. He said I might be in a delirium, and I don't know whether I was or not. He said that before he died, Bucko Breen had spoken of a pink macaw, and it was that same night I was attacked. That was real enough, for I still bear the scars. And I will swear the bird had blood on its beak and talons when it came through that window.

"But I am afraid of what will come next. I am helpless, and I can trust no one. I don't know whether the servants are his men or not. The doctor and you—I can trust no one else. He has told me that I am poisoned, that my life is going slowly, and that only he can provide the antidote. He has got from me a power of attorney, which has enabled him to ruin me.

"Everything which was mine is now his. He knows of the compact between me and Pindar, and he threatens to expose me to the marine underwriters— even while I am ill. Years ago he swore a vendetta against me, and this is the result. If I were up and about I would fight him, even if I lost; but I am a stricken man and a beaten one.

"It is as a last hope I have asked you to come to see me, Sexton Blake. I have kept nothing back. You know now that most of the things they said about Bully Blood were true enough. But I cannot pass out like this! I appeal to you to save me! I appeal to you to meet that merciless dog who calls himself the Black Eagle and to beat him. I swear to you that if you do I shall make whatever restitution lies in my power. Give me a chance to make up for the past and redeem my soul.

"Lying here, I have seen things in a different light, and now I know what an evil thing I was. But my repentance is a true repentance, and I want a chance to wipe out the evil past before I go before the Judgment Seat. Will you help me? I live here in hourly terror!

"I know not at what moment he will strike again, or in what way. Before he left me he swore that within three days he would strike again, and that when he did it would be the finishing blow. Even at this moment he may be coming! I—cannot —bear—beg you— beseech you—"

And then what shreds of control he had retained snapped entirely as he broke down, heaving with choking sobs, a completely unmanned creature for whom, even in his contempt and realisation that his punishment was no more than just, Blake could not help having some pity. As the man grew quieter, he leant over and talked to him soothingly. Then, when the other was quiet again, he said:

"It is just because you have confessed all and feel a true remorse that I am going to do what I can to help you. If I succeed, then I shall hold you to your promise to make every restitution in your power, and to live in the future in a way that will compensate for the past. Now compose yourself, for I have a few questions to ask you."

And as the man regained his control, Blake proceeded with his interrogation.

CHAPTER 4.   A Definite Move—And Desperate Action.

IT was well after his usual lunch-hour when Blake left the house in Upper Brook Street and walked into Park Lane, where he got a taxi. He drove through to Baker Street at once, where he found Tinker having his lunch.

Over the meal Blake gave the lad details of what had occurred since he had gone off with Dr. Green, and then, when they were back once more in the consulting-room, he said:

"I can't tell just what is going to be the upshot of all this, my lad. One thing, however, is plain, and that is that the Black Eagle is carrying on a deadly vendetta against Gore—or Bully Blood, as we know him best. If it were a person of less daring than the Black Eagle, I should be inclined to discount a good deal that Blood has said, and to put it down to the excited condition of his mind, attendant upon his belief that he is a stricken man—which he seems to be at that.

"But we know the calibre of the Black Eagle too well to minimise any of his threats, and certainly, from what I can gather, he seems to have planned this whole affair with extraordinary care. A man like the Black Eagle does not spend months of drudgery in a subordinate position in the City for nothing. I know that he is extremely well off, and he must have had some very strong motive for doing so.

"I told you at the time what had taken place that night at the baccarat game, and also of the strange death of Bucko Breen, in the East End. That there is a very strong connection between the two I am now convinced, and I suspected as much at the time.

"There is a good deal of mystery to be cleared up about this pink macaw, which enters into the affair so often. Blood is in such a state that he doesn't know whether to believe in the actual existence of the bird, or whether it is all a figment of his imagination, despite the scars which still remain of the other attack. And the Black Eagle has played on this point to the extreme.

"But what is at least sufficiently concrete for us is the Black Eagle's very definite threat, which he made to Blood the night before last. On that occasion he swore that within three days he would strike his last blow, but he gave no hint as to how it would come. He simply told Blood that at a time and in a way that he least expected he would strike, and that, together with the fear of death which is on the man, has unnerved him completely.

96

"I must say that Blood thoroughly deserved all that was said about him in the past. He has confessed as much to me. But at the moment he is filled with remorse, and is in such a panic that he vows solemnly that if I will save him he will live but to make restitution for his sins of the past. That in itself is a strong point in his favour; and, further, if the Black Eagle told him the truth the night before last, then Blood's illness is due to a very subtle poison which the Black Eagle introduced into his drink the night of the baccarat party.

"As a matter of fact, now that I recall the occasion, I can see that this would have been a simple matter, for the Black Eagle and his brother served the wine and sandwiches, and it could have been done easily then, for all the others at the table were discussing the game.

"We have been up against the Black Eagle before, and on the last occasion I gave him a definite warning. I cannot stand by and see him complete this subtle and terrible vengeance on Blood without lifting a hand to help the man.

"Besides, there is the question of the fraud on the marine underwriters to put right, and at the moment all those monies are in the hands of the Black Eagle. So it seems, my lad, that once again, even in the rush of other things, we shall have to take up the gage and go after him."

"That suits me all right, guv'nor," said Tinker, with a grin. "One thing is certain—if we do buck the Black Eagle, we are sure to get a run for our money, and that is more than we had in this last case we just finished. That is," he added hastily, "if I get a look-in."

Blake smiled.

"You will get that all right," he rejoined grimly. "In fact, I have picked out a leading part for you, and I want you to go off at once!"

"What is it, sir?" asked the lad eagerly, jumping to his feet.

"I am appointing you special bodyguard to Bully Blood. You will go to Upper Brook Street now, and there you will be shown into his bed-room. You will take up your post there, and be ready to take action if anything out of the ordinary occurs. I can't give you a hint of what that may be. Perhaps nothing will happen. But you are to be ready, and I am going to hold you responsible for Blood's safety until I relieve you. Take your most dependable weapon, and, if circumstances force you to use it, then do so, and you will know that I take the responsibility.

"Talk to no one there, but just take up your guard and stick to it.

Blood says he mistrusts even his own servants, but I don't know. The male nurses may be crooked, but you will probably be able to discover that. At any rate, don't let yourself be bluffed, and remember that from the moment you take over you are in supreme charge of the sick-room. You will, of course, do or say nothing to excite the patient, and discourage any attempt of his to talk. Do you understand?"

"Perfectly, sir. Don't worry! I'll go on the job and stick there, and if there is any hanky-panky afoot, I'll tackle it. Shall I go along at once?"

"Yes. And remain there until you hear from me. I am going to tackle the Black Eagle by direct action, and I do not know what the result may be, or whither it may lead me. When you do hear from me, it will either be in person or in some way you can't mistake. Pay no heed to anything else, no matter how genuine it may seem. Now be off!"

Ten minutes later Tinker took his departure, and when he did so he was just a little better equipped than Blake had instructed him to be, for, instead of one gun he packed two—his main standby being a big .45 service revolver, and, as an auxiliary for quick snap-shooting, a handy little .32 automatic which had served him well in the past.

As for Blake, he turned off a certain amount of work until he saw that it was tea-time; then he rang for his tea, and after that donned his coat and hat to make his way Citywards.

His first call was at the Royal Exchange, where he had a half-hour's conversation with a certain underwriter, from whom he gained quite a lot of valuable information regarding recent marine policies issued through the various underwriting syndicates of Lloyds.

It was almost five o'clock when Blake left the Royal Exchange, and taxied straight through to Fenchurch Street, where the offices of the Gore Shipping Line were situated.

He dismissed his taxi there, and, after a brief bit of scouting round, found a convenient position where he could take up his stand and keep an eye on the home-going workers, who were already beginning to emerge from the great, gloomy looking hives of business which lined the street.

He took occasion then, too, to hail a passing taxi and bargain with the man to wait at the kerb, in case he should need him, and, a little later on, he was glad he had had the forethought to do so. He was at his post nearly half an hour, when at last he sighted his quarry.

Even in the guise of David Burr, there was no question in Blake's mind of the identity of his man. It was the Black Eagle himself; and, as he watched the brisk, alert passage of the man across the footpath to a big car which was waiting, Blake had to confess that, physically as well as mentally, he was an opponent to be reckoned with not lightly.

The moment the Black Eagle was inside the waiting car Blake made for his taxi, and, after giving the driver instructions to follow the other vehicle, but not too closely, he jumped in and they were off.

The trail was not a difficult one to follow, for his driver seemed to have no difficulty in keeping the other car in sight all through the City and past the Bank towards the West End. Along Victoria Street they went, and then into Cannon Street; from there past St. Paul's and down Ludgate Hill to the Circus; thence up Fleet Street, past the Law Courts and Aldwych, and into the Strand, where they ran into one traffic block after another.

One occasion, Blake, who was peering ahead through the window, feared they had lost their quarry, for it managed to get past the uplifted arm of the constable on point duty just as their taxi was held up. But fortunately, the block was a brief one, and, putting on speed, Blake's driver again brought the other vehicle in sight by the time they were running into Trafalgar Square.

It was an easy chase from there. Along Pall Mall and up Lower Regent Street, then across Piccadilly Circus into the Regent Quadrant, and so on to Oxford Street; and, when they had turned up that vast thoroughfare in the direction of the Marble Arch, Blake began to have a shrewd idea as to the Black Eagle's destination.

When the car ahead turned into the Edgware Road he felt certain, and, as the taxi also took the same turning, Blake lifted his hand and tapped on the window with his knuckles. The taxi slowed down, and, opening the door a trifle, Blake told the man to go along slowly and to stop when he should rap again.

They continued in this way until Blake saw the other vehicle turn off into what he knew was the street leading to the crescent, and as they reached the corner he tapped again.

Springing out, he told the man to wait, and, without giving the other time to raise an objection, he swung round the corner and walked at a brisk pace into the crescent. He made his way straight across it until he came to the iron railing which enclosed a small plot of dingy green turf and trees, the branches of which were bare at that time of year.

He kept close to the railing until he had reached a point from which he could observe the house on the corner which he knew was occupied by the man who called himself David Stone, and there he stopped.

As he had hoped, there was a big car standing at the kerb outside the door which gave access from the side street, and Blake knew that he had run his man to earth.

What the Black Eagle might be planning to do next, he could not guess, but he was determined to keep up his vigil until he should discover if he intended making a move that evening, or if he had gone to earth for the night.

He paid no attention to the few pedestrians who passed through the crescent from time to time, but the second time a constable came by, peering at him suspiciously, Blake thought it best to disclose his identity to the officer, as he did not wish his plans to be upset by any complications in that direction.

He said as little as was necessary, which wasn't much when the constable knew it was the famous detective who was on the prowl, and, although he probably felt a keen curiosity to know just what was afoot, the latter did not ask any questions. He loitered about the place for a bit, on the watch to see if anything should happen; but as the time passed, and the chill of the November night began to penetrate through even his thick greatcoat, he moved off in the direction of the next street, to continue his beat.

And all this time Blake had been praying fervently that the man might have some objective in some other street where, perchance, a good-natured cook had a hot tit-bit waiting for him.

And with the departure of the constable Blake seemed to have the whole crescent to himself. Still, he stuck it out, although he knew from his watch that it was now after eight o'clock.

So far, not a sign had come from the house on the corner, but he thought he could vaguely make out the form of a man sitting behind the wheel of the big car, and from that he figured it looked as if the Black Eagle might again make use of it.

Just then he heard the sound of another motor vehicle, and, glancing towards the Edgware Road, he saw what he took to be his own waiting taxi turn the corner slowly.

"The man is getting worried," he thought. "He thinks I have bilked him. Confound him, anyway. It means I shall have to leave my post and stop him before he gets into the crescent."

He made his way swiftly round by the iron railings, and then, keeping to the shadow of the buildings, moved cautiously until he was out of sight of the man in the other car. Then he started to run, and reached the oncoming taxi just before it reached the corner of the crescent.

He stopped the man with uplifted hand, and, stepping into the road, shot a few remarks at him, which gave the fellow one of the biggest surprises he ever got in his life. It did not serve that he protested that he had no idea of the identity of his fare and thought he had run off and left him. Blake was savage at the risk of having his plans upset, and, after curtly ordering the man back to wait where he had been told, he turned and once move started back across the crescent.

He was again making for the iron rails, and had just come in sight of the big car, when suddenly he saw a figure cross the pavement swiftly. It was a big, bulky form, and looked to Blake like the Black Eagle. He appeared to be carrying some sort of burden in his hand, for the silhouette bulked considerably by his knees.

That was all Blake had time to observe before the other disappeared inside the waiting car, and the next moment something struck the asphalt paving so close to Blake's feet that the toe of his shoe was ticked in the passage of the object. Almost at the same moment came the sound of a faint "ping," and Blake drew up with a jerk.

"That was a bullet," was the thought that crossed his mind like a flash. "A bullet, and it came from that house on the corner. It was fired out of an air gun, or a gun with a silencer attached. It—"

But just then another bullet flipped between his legs, passing clean through the loose fold of his trousers, and with that Blake turned and made for the corner which he had just left. At the same time the big car came thundering through the crescent, almost bowling him over in its course, and, as it passed, from an open window, something came hurtling which caught Blake on the shoulder with terrific force, and sent him staggering to one side, half-dazed from the impact.

The object clattered to his feet, and as he recovered himself he bent to pick it up. It was a heavy spanner, which the occupant of the car had hurled at him in passing, and Blake knew now without a doubt that he had been spotted from the house while he had been standing by the iron rails in the crescent.

By now the big car was out of sight round the corner. It had turned up the Edgware Road, and as he realised how nearly those two bullets and the spanner had done for him, a cold rage filled Blake.

Clutching the spanner, he began to run. He rounded the corner, to find the taxi waiting where he had instructed the man to pull up. He jerked open the door as he reached it, and said, while still on the jump:

"That same car—just gone up the road— after it, and don't lose it on you life!"

Then he was inside, and as the door slammed the taxi was off with a jerk, turning almost on two wheels. If Blake wanted action the peeved taxi driver intended giving it to him.

They passed the Marble Arch at a terrific pace, and swung down into Park Lane without slackening speed, but, even at that, the big car was well ahead of them, and when it finally disappeared from view it was only Blake's knowledge of the house in Upper Brook Street that told him it had taken that turning. He jerked open the door and shouted to the driver the number of Gore's house, and then it seemed just a few moments later they took the corner at a bound, and the taxi came into the kerb with a loud shrieking of brakes.

There was no need then for Blake to ask which way the other vehicle had gone. It was standing at the kerb directly in front of Gore's house, and as he struck the pavement Blake paused for a moment at the astounding sight which met his gaze.

At first everything had seemed quiet and normal enough, and he had thought the Black Eagle had already gained access to the house. But then his eyes went upwards, and he saw a blurred figure clinging to the stone railing of the big porch over the front steps.

In the same moment he saw the man jerk out his arm, and in the dim light Blake saw what seemed to be a giant bird sweep up, flutter with a tremendous flapping of wings as if suddenly confused at finding itself abroad in the night, then it turned, and, with a raucous screech, hurled itself through a half-open window at one side of the porch.

It was the window giving on to the bedroom occupied by Barnfield Gore, and at the moment when the pink macaw disappeared (for Blake knew now that it was indeed that devil in feathers which had been brought to the place by the Black Eagle in a bag) a high-pitched scream of terror reached him.

The next moment the Black Eagle himself came slithering down the pillar of the porch, and as he struck the top steps he caught sight of Blake.

He waited just a second or so to take in the scene, then he came down the steps on the run; and he was no more eager than Sexton Blake, for the detective had already gathered himself together, was keeping well in his mind the full danger of those deadly hands of the other, and then—the pair crashed.

Not a word was said. Whether the Black Eagle and his brother had guessed Blake's identity while he was standing by the iron rails in the crescent, Blake did not know or care. That the hunchback had taken a couple of pot-shots at him while the Black Eagle got away he did know. But if the Black Eagle hadn't known then, he knew now, and his teeth showed in a snarl as he tried to break through Blake's guard and get his hands on his throat.

But Sexton Blake was no boasting swashbuckler such as Captain Pindar. On the contrary. He was one of the most finished exponents of the art of fighting to be met with. It was one of the most important needs of the dangerous profession he followed that he should keep himself iron-hard all the time, and that he should be master of every style of fighting which prevailed.

No one realised better than Blake just how short his shrift would be once the Black Eagle got those deadly hands on his throat. He had never forgotten the feat of strength he had once seen the other perform in a moment of abstraction, and he knew his only chance was to keep the other at a distance and make him fight a stand-up battle. The Black Eagle sensed this quick enough, and for the time at least he made to play Blake's game. He saw that Blake's guard was too sure a block for him to get under while Blake was looking for those tactics, and, being nothing loth to mix it in any fashion, he stood toe to toe with his man.

And there in that exclusive street in London's night began a fight that would have put to shame the average heavy-weight contest which the long-suffering, fight-loving public pays its money to see staged.

They were both big men, and the thud of their blows could be heard in deadly beat as they drove in again and again and again, each seeking to batter down the other's guard and find a weak point on which to follow up.

So swiftly had the combat started that the taxi-driver and the man behind the wheel of the Black Eagle's car were scarcely aware what was happening before the two fighters were well mixed.

What had happened or was happening in the sick-room above Blake didn't know. But he knew the mental condition of the patient, and he would guess pretty well what effect the eerie appearance of the screeching pink macaw would have on him just then.

It had been almost a superstitious fear with him that the bird would appear again; and Blake realised that the Black Eagle could not have chosen a more subtle or more effective means of striking than that. He had counted on Blood being alone at the time, or that the only other person with him would be one of the male nurses. He had known nothing of Tinker's presence in the room, and Blake knew Tinker would have to deal with the bird quickly if he were to counteract the effect it would have on Blood.

But that was about all the time he could give to a consideration of that phase of the matter. Once he did think he heard the sound of a pistol-shot, and the Black Eagle must have heard the same sound, for, as if it had started him wondering, he eased up a little in his attack, and involuntarily stepped back.

But Blake was into the opening like a tiger, and, with a terrific right to the body, drove the Black Eagle against the foot of the steps, and, before he could recover, followed him with a short, vicious left that caught him clean and full on the point of the jaw.

The Black Eagle's foot struck the lower step, and Blake was in the very act of trying to send in another blow as the finishing touch, when suddenly something struck him on the arm with paralysing force, and, as he staggered round to see what it was, he found the driver of the Black Eagle's car raising his arm for a second blow.

In his hand was a heavy spanner, and this he had driven down with all his strength on Blake's biceps. For the moment Blake's right arm was useless except as a feeble guard, and as he recovered himself the Black Eagle came on with a rush. For the moment Blake was helpless to put up any sort of defence, and he told himself that this time those terrible hands must find his throat. But even as they were reaching out something intervened, and this time it was the Black Eagle who staggered aside.

Blake turned swiftly and found his own taxi-driver also wielding a heavy spanner, and as he sent the Black Eagle back he grunted "Fair play, or no fight. Start that spanner business again and I'll brain the pair of you. My man was getting the best of it until you started that. Now, you murderous dog, get back and let them go!"

But the man who had reached Blake's side so opportunely was not to have his lust of battle satisfied just then, for before it could be renewed there came the sound of heavy footsteps, and down the street came the burly form of a constable.

Even before he reached them he was beginning to ask what it was all about, and as he caught sight of him the Black Eagle grabbed the arm of his driver and rushed him towards the car. The man jumped for the seat while the Black Eagle flung open the door and sprang inside, and, while Blake was just turning to try and take some means of stopping them, the big car gave a roar and went off down the street with a jerk.

Blake would have followed in the taxi, but the constable had him by the arm, and by the time he had furiously explained matters to that conscientious officer, the fugitive vehicle was out of sight.

Blake was inwardly raging as he finally convinced the constable and bade him follow him up the steps. His hand was just reaching for the bell when he heard sounds of rapid footsteps inside, and the door was jerked open as the footman came out on the run, a police-whistle at his lips.

Blake, instead of touching the bell-button, shot up his hand and jerked the whistle from the clutch of the man, and pushed him inside, followed by the constable and the taxi-driver.

And just as they stepped into the hall there came a wild clatter overhead, and the next moment two figures, tightly locked together, came hurtling down the stairs to hit the polished floor at the bottom with a crash that caused the pictures on the wall to bump and sway.

From the tangle Blake saw Tinker scramble to his feet, and, after one swift glance, he started forward with an exclamation of concern, for the lad's face was literally covered with blood, and, as he raised his hands, Blake saw that they, too, were streaked with fresh crimson.

Tinker saw him, and started towards him. It was plain that he was fighting hard to control his reeling senses, and, as Blake sprang towards him he heard the lad mutter:

"That—bird—guv'nor—couldn't shoot but once—saved Blood,

but the devil got me again and again—can't see for blood—then the nurse came in and rushed me—knew I had to keep going until you came—hope it is all—" And with that he collapsed in Blake's arms.

CHAPTER 5. A Terrific Fight.

BY the time Blake had got to work on Tinker with a basin of hot water and soft cloths he found that the lad's injuries were not as serious as had appeared from the quantity of blood which had been drawn.

Blake had left the nurse to the care of the constable, who had rung through for an ambulance when he found the man's legs were both broken, and that he was suffering from internal injuries as well.

But that the lad had had a terrific battle with the giant macaw was evident, and, when consciousness returned, he insisted on telling Blake what had happened.

"I was on guard," he said weakly, "just as you had instructed me. Nothing happened all afternoon. The doctor came about five, but didn't ask me any questions. So I said nothing. The day nurse came in a few times, and then, at eight o'clock, the night nurse came on duty. I didn't like the cut of either of them, and kept a close watch when they were in the room. Blood tried to talk once or twice, but I told him my instructions were to guard him, and not to answer questions, so he shut up.

"Then that thing came through the open window. There wasn't a sign or sound of anything. It just swept in, like a ghost, with one screech, and Blood let out a yell of terror. I was sitting by the bed, and had my automatic in the side-pocket of my coat, ready for business. The bird was more like a devil than anything else.

"It was uncanny the way it came in, and it made straight for Blood. I jerked out my gun, and took one pot shot at it; but I daren't shoot again, for fear of hitting Blood. He was in an awful state, and I managed to throw myself on my back across the bed just before the bird struck. I tried to defend myself, but the thing got me with its beak and claws again and again, until I managed to get one of the pillows free and use it as a shield.

"Then I worked my way on to the floor, and the macaw seemed to transfer its attack to me. I don't want a fight like that again, guv'nor. It was the quickest thing I have ever tackled. It was in and out like lightning, and it managed to mark me every time. I could see it was after my eyes or my throat, and I knew it would blind me, sure, if I didn't 'get' it first. I had to let it gouge me pretty badly to do so, but at last I grabbed it, and, once I had got hold of it, I hung on.

"It fought like a fury. Honest, it seemed half human and half fiend, guv'nor. But I hung on, and at last I got my fingers on its throat. And then—then I throttled the life out of it, guv'nor. But the thing struggled to the very last.

"I had just finished it off when the night nurse rushed in, and, without a word, went for me. That was the sort of fighting I understood, but before I could get my gun into action he was upon me, so I couldn't use it. I don't know just what happened then. I remember finding myself outside the room then, at the top of the stairs, and after that we both came down. That is all, guv'nor. I was trying to keep things under until you turned up, but I did not know you were near. Did you find the Black Eagle?"

"I found him," answered Blake. "And you did splendidly, my lad! Now lie here quietly for a few minutes. I want to go upstairs."

Blake turned then, and ran up the stairs to the sick-room. He found Bully Blood huddled under the clothes, almost frantic with terror; but Blake caught him by the shoulder, and shook him roughly.

"No time for that now!" he said harshly. "If I am to help you, you must do something to help yourself."

"The bird—the pink macaw!" came a moan.

For answer, Blake ran round the bed, where he found the body of the pink macaw. All over the room were pink and indigo feathers, which had flown about during the awful fight between it and Tinker. Blake picked the still warm carcase up, and forced Blood to look at it.

"There is your pink macaw," he said curtly. "It will never worry you again."

"Then it was real," whispered Blood, staring at it in fascination.

"Real? Of course, it was real!" snorted Blake. "Touch it, man, and see for yourself. The Black Eagle was just playing on your fears. I met him just as he sent the bird through the open window. He has got away for the time being, but I am going after him. I want your promise that you will keep quiet until I return, and not give way to this sort of terror. It is your only hope, and I promise you that, if I do find the Black Eagle, I shall bring back with me the antidote of this poison which is in you, or I shall not come back at all. Here, take this revolver of mine, and it will make you feel safer."

With that, Blake turned and made for the door. He closed it after him, and ran down the stairs. In the lower hall he encountered the constable, and, after a few words with him, set him on guard inside the door. Then he found the footman, and sent him up to the sick room, to inform his master that the constable was in the house, and that he himself would remain in the room with him.

Then he went to Tinker, and found the lad sitting on the edge of a couch, feeling more like himself.

"Will you remain here until I return, my lad?" asked Blake. "I think it would be better."

"Where are you going, guv'nor?"

"After the Black Eagle!" answered Blake curtly.

"Then I'm coming, too," insisted Tinker, as he got to his feet. "I'm not feeling so bad—honest, guv'nor. That blamed bird dragged out a lot of blood, but there is nothing really deep. I must come with you."

"All right." answered Blake. "But first give me one of your weapons. I think you said you had two."

Tinker drew out the big Service revolver and the automatic, and offered Blake his choice. Blake selected the larger, and then the pair made for the front door, just inside which the taxi-driver was standing, talking to the constable. Blake signed to him to follow, and they went down the steps on the run.

Pausing by the cab, Blake told the man, who was now as keen as a terrier to follow up the street, to drive back to the crescent off the Edgware Road, and, when Tinker had stumbled in, he followed.

But this time Blake had the taxi drawn up at a different spot. He rapped on the window, and the man drew in to the kerb at the corner just before the one which Blake had previously turned. It was Blake's intention to get to the house on the corner of the crescent by the side road leading from the other direction, and as soon as he was out of the cab he started off.

The driver wanted to come along, but Blake shook his head. What he had to do that night he was determined to do singlehanded, if Tinker could not help him, and, while the lad might be of some use with a gun, even that was problematical, for both hands were swathed in bandages, and only the ends of his fingers stuck out.

They made their way round the first corner, and kept on until they came to the next. Here Blake turned sharply to the right, and just ahead of them lay the crescent, while on the far corner on their right was the house which was their objective.

Blake seemed a little puzzled as he saw there was no car outside, and he drew up to take a survey before proceeding.

"Something queer about that," he said, in a low tone, to Tinker. "I had counted on the Black Eagle making straight back here. It is going to complicate matters for us if he has gone to earth some other place. He knew it was I who tackled him in Upper Brook Street, and he may have counted on my coming here after him. But I don't know. He may already have gone to earth inside, and sent the car off. But I can scarcely believe he would leave himself without some such means for a quick getaway, if necessary. And I am sure he did not know I was on his trail until I tackled him. Therefore, it does not seem reasonable to think that he already had his plans for taking flight. He could not foresee what was going to take place to-night. Whether to wait outside for him or to try and gain access to the place—that is the problem, my lad."

"He's a canny bird all right," remarked Tinker. "Why not take a chance on getting inside, guv'nor? It will either bring things to a show-down, or we shall know that he is already on the wing."

"I agree, my lad. I think we will tackle the thing as you say. Keep that gun of yours handy, but don't use it unless you have to. We don't know what we shall find in there—if we get in. But if it is necessary to shoot, then we shall do so. And don't forget that hunchback brother of his. He has the strength of a gorilla, and I have an idea he has already taken a couple of snap-shots at me this evening. Come on and watch your step."

With that Blake again started forward, with Tinker close by his side. They kept on until they came to the side door, which was the only apparent entrance to that queer house, and, lifting his hand, Blake pressed the bell.

They stood waiting for some minutes, but could hear no sounds within, and Blake was just on the point of ringing again when, without the slightest warning, the door swung open.. Blake did not pause, although he knew not what sort of trap might be waiting inside. Instead, he got his shoulder against the door and smashed it full back while he entered, followed by Tinker.

At first he could see no one, but that there must be someone to work the secret mechanism of the door was evident, for no sooner were they inside than it slammed after them.

Blake moved forward through the lobby and into the lounge hall until he could command a view of the stairs, and, just as he gazed upwards, he caught sight of the hunchback at the top.

In that moment Blake read the truth. It was not they who had been expected but the Black Eagle. That secret mechanism had been pressed for the owner of the house, and not for them. He could read in the strange yellow eyes and swaying movement of the strange gorilla-like figure above as the creature struggled to understand just what had happened, and to decide how he should deal with it.

And, as Blake had feared, he went at once to the primitive. He had just time to give a quick warning to Tinker that the hunchback was going to attack, and to say: "We must try and overpower him without hurting him, for he is irresponsible," when the great burly figure came crashing down the stairs, and in the low crouch which brought the hairy fists almost to the floor, looked more like a great ape than ever.

As he came bounding across the lounge he gave utterance to strange sounds which Blake and Tinker could not understand, but which they read as incoherent signs of a deep rage, and in that moment, as Blake rushed to meet him he knew that those tawny eyes were filled with the savage determination to kill him.

There could be no question of explanations with this strange bit of mis-shapen humanity. He was just a primitive cave creature in a crazed rage, and as that he must be dealt with. And yet, the handicap which Blake carried was that he must conquer without doing vital injury. If he failed—if he missed a single move—his neck would be snapped like the clay stem of a pipe—and he knew it.

There was no method or reason in the other's attack. Just like the giant ape which he resembled, he came in with lips apart, drooling from the corners of his mouth and drumming, drumming, drumming on his great chest. The sound, in those enclosed four walls, was like the dull hammering of a muffled tom-tom.

The barrel of the creatures ribs was enormous, and Blake knew that once he was drawn in against it he would have the life crushed out of him as quickly as a grizzly would have given him the death hug.

Nor could he hope to use his fists in the ordinary way. He might win a victory if he could connect with his left to the point of the chin, but no strength he possessed nor punch of man could make any impression on that tree-like torso. Tinker was standing at one side, wary as a cat.

He had pulled out his automatic, and was holding it clumsily with both hands. He knew perfectly well what he had to do. He knew just as well as Blake that he must not vitally injure the strange creature, and yet he knew he must be prepared to shoot to bring his man down if Blake went under.

Even at the risk of killing, he was determined to do that rather than see Blake go too close to the verge of death. And then they crashed.

The hunchback had stopped drumming on his chest, and with an agility which was almost unbelievable had thrown his arms wide and was in on Blake. Only a lightning-like dodge at the last moment saved Blake from that terrible embrace, and as he swung to one side he drove in his left, with a jolt that shook the hunchback and stopped him short in his rush.

He gave his head a shake and emitted a grunt as he felt the impact, but that was the most it seemed to affect him, and again he came on with the same stupid manner and the same baffling speed of movement.

Blake kept moving back slowly, giving ground first to one side and then to the other. On the second rush he was more on the alert, and this time, as the hunchback missed him, Blake brought his right round in a short sweep, and, with all the force of his shoulder behind, it got home just under the other's torn ear.

And it was then Blake knew he had found a weak spot, for the hunchback emitted a sharp cry of agony as Blake's fist connected. The thought flashed into Blake's mind that it was possible that at the time that ear had been so brutally torn away, a deeper injury had been done which had left some vital part of the inner skull unprotected, and at this he set himself to concentrate on that spot.

Now it was he who became the more active. Until then, he had been more on the defensive, but as he cleared the low tabourette in the centre of the room he quickened his footwork, and was in and out with a speed which he could see was baffling the hunchback. He had found the secret, and he was riding it while he could, for none knew better than he that it was his only hope.

That first blow under the ear had done deeper damage than Blake thought, and, so agonising had been the pain, that, although Blake only dimly guessed the truth, the hunchback had been nothing but a confused automaton from that moment. Some primitive instinct had driven him on, but what little reasoning power he possessed had been stupefied, and, as Blake continued to hammer away at that same vital spot, the hunchback's brain ceased almost completely to function.

He showed little signs of it outwardly, however. To all appearances, he was as dangerous as ever, and again and again he swept those great arms round with a speed that more than once almost caught Blake in their embrace.

But as a fighter Blake was as sensitive as a panther, and it was this instinct he was now following. Something inside him told him to keep on at that spot under the ear, and as he bored in time after time, the watching Tinker knew that in some way Blake had found what he had been seeking and was making the most of it.

But the fight was not over yet. Round and round the lounge they went crashing, now the hunchback rushing and Blake retreating, and then Blake, with a marvellous speed beautiful to watch, boring in and tapping, tapping that same spot.

Over near the foot of the stairs the hunchback made a change in his tactics. There he stumbled against the bottom step, and that seemed to bring his brain into play again, for he sprang backwards and upwards, to land on the fourth step, and then, before Blake could gather just what his intention was, he came plunging downwards in a clean leap for Blake's shoulders.

How Blake slipped under at the last moment he never could have told—nor could Tinker. For one terrible moment the lad thought Blake was going down, then he saw the sturdy shoulders emerge, saw Blake shoot his left out as if it was governed by a steel spring, saw the right flash after it, then the hunchback gave a great cry and staggered away, groping like a blind creature.

And that is exactly what had happened to him. Blake's last blow had touched some inward nerve which had caused the temporary paralysis to shoot along to the eyes, and now he was as helpless as any Cyclops of fable as he went lumbering helplessly about the room.

Blake followed up his advantage swiftly. He dragged down curtain cords, and once he had a loop about the hunchback's arms he knew he had him where he wanted him. Then, with Tinker's assistance, he bound him hand and foot, and finished the job by gagging him.

Together they dragged him along to the studio, and had just deposited him on the floor there when, as they stepped back into the lounge, the whirr of a bell sounded, and somehow Blake knew that the Black Eagle had returned. And the same instinct told him that this time his life and Tinker's were in deadly jeopardy.

CHAPTER 6.   The Antidote—Conclusion.

SEXTON BLAKE had no fear of what was to come, but he would have been better pleased if it had come later. He had already had a strenuous doing that evening, what with his fight with the Black Eagle in Upper Brook Street and the more recent battle with the hunchback. Where the Black Eagle had gone after his flight from Upper Brook Street he did not know, but he felt almost certain that the person now ringing at the door was he, and, even if he tried to gain time by not opening, he knew that would not avail, for it was certain the owner of the house would have a key of his own.

From what he had observed, he had seen that there were two means of releasing the lock from within—one being in the ordinary way by turning the knob of the spring lock inside, and the other which had been employed on occasion by the hunchback when on the floor above.

If Blake had only known where to find this second button, he would have gone upstairs and taken that point of vantage before opening the door. But he did not know its location, and just then he had no time to look. The only thing to do was to meet the situation as it had developed, and to strike, if possible, before the Black Eagle.

He took a rapid survey of the place, then he motioned for Tinker to take up his position on the stairs.

"Keep your gun ready!" he whispered. "I don't know how this is going to work out! The Black Eagle will be killing mad when he comes in, for he is bound to know that something has happened to his brother. If I go under, then shoot—but not unless that happens."

Just then the bell rang again, and as Tinker made for the stairs Blake strode from the lounge into the lobby and laid his fingers on the knob of the spring lock.

He stood well behind the door before opening it, then he gave the knob a turn, and drew it in abruptly and yet smoothly, just as he had seen it swing inwards when the hunchback had pressed the release button on the upper floor.

The next instant the Black Eagle himself crossed the threshold, and started through the lobby; but as he reached the door leading into the lounge hall he paused, and Blake knew he was suspiciously surveying the wreckage in that apartment.

It was then that Blake struck. From where he had been standing, he covered the distance in a couple of long strides, and, gathering his muscles taut, sprang. He landed on the Black Eagle's back, and the terrific force of his impetus carried them both through the doorway and half across the lounge in the direction of the tabourette, which was lying on its side, where it had been knocked over in the previous struggle.

As Blake struck him the Black Eagle gave a gasp, and as he staggered to a stop in the lounge, he brought his powerful arms up in a backward sweep to try and counter the hold by which Blake had got him.

The Black Eagle needed no telling as to what had happened. Straight in front of him was a big mirror, and, looking into that, he could see the grim countenance of the detective over his shoulder. And if the Black Eagle's hands were deadly in the throttle, the long, muscular fingers which Blake was digging into his jugular now were almost as terrible.

One of Blake's legs was curled round that of the Black Eagle, and in this sort of hold Blake was undoubtedly the superior, for it was an old wrestling hold that he had used again and again with deadly effect. Even with Blake's fingers in his throat, the Black Eagle paused for a few seconds after his first abortive attempt to reach up and break the hold.

For the moment his mind was more exercised over what could have happened to his brother than over his own danger. He knew now that in his absence Blake had gained access to the place, and that something had put his brother out of the way.

On escaping from Upper Brook Street, he would have made direct for the house in the crescent had it not been that he had certain things to do in Fenchurch Street before making his getaway. From Fenchurch Street he could have made straight for the coast, but he had driven back west in order to warn his brother, and in that way had walked straight into Blake's arms. And in doing that he had brought with him in his pocket the very things which Sexton Blake was seeking, although Blake didn't know that at the time.

All this in that brief pause while Blake consolidated his position, so to speak; then the Black Eagle's roving eye spotted Tinker on the stairs. In the same moment there came to him the sharp realisation that he was in a very nasty place, and that those deadly fingers at his throat would soon make short work of him if he didn't break their hold soon.

And at this he seemed to go berserk. His body stiffened suddenly, as if every muscle was governed by a steel spring. Then he bent, and there began a mighty fight for supremacy between those two, each of whom was a past master in every phase of the game.

Tinker watched it with a fascinated gaze. He had seen Blake in a good many fights, and the battle with the hunchback had been no mean "go." He had watched him stand up and batter down one Dr. Huxton Rymer, than whom there were few, if any, better exponents of "rila-tila" fighting living. But he had never seen Blake in a fight that resolved itself into such a deadly, sinister battle as on this occasion, when he fought for supremacy and life with the Black Eagle.

In a swift turn, the Black Eagle managed to swing round, and then, despite Blake's, efforts, he forced his way back and back until he had almost reached the big, open fireplace, where a heap of logs was burning. Blake managed to shift his position then, but with a heave the Black Eagle got back another foot or so, and this time he jammed Blake's limbs into the flames.

Blake had to let go. No one but a fanatical savage could have withstood those licking tongues of flame, and as he broke free the Black Eagle came round with a snarl like a tiger, and the pair drove in like two wild men.

From that on, it was a ding-dong battle, with each employing every atom of fighting art he possessed. Around and around the lounge they went, crashing into tables and chairs, and creating havoc in their passage.

More than once Tinker made as if to take a hand, or at least to use his gun, but he knew Blake would give him "gippo" —as the lad would have put it—if he had done so. Therefore he watched, ready if need be.

It seemed that the two must have been battling for more than a quarter of an hour when, as the Black Eagle was giving ground in his turn, Blake drove him full against the door leading to the studio. It crashed inwards, and both went clean through into the other apartment.

They must have lurched back against the door immediately they were inside, for it slammed hard, and when Tinker ran across and tried to enter he could not make it move.

On another occasion, at the time Blake had first come in contact with the Black Eagle, Tinker had been overpowered by the hunchback, and had been held prisoner in that same house. On that occasion he had seen part of the upper floor, for he had been confined in the same small room which had recently housed the pink macaw.

And at that time he had noticed, through the open door at the end of the passage, the gallery which ran round high up in the studio, and on a level with the upper floor. This came to his mind now, and, turning, he sped swiftly up the stairs.

He raced along the hall there and opened the door at the end. He stepped out on to the balcony, and, looking down, saw the battling pair beneath.

Even as he watched, he saw Blake brace himself, and then the rug on which his foot was resting slid from under him, and he went down on one knee. The Black Eagle was on him like a panther, and before Blake could recover himself those terrible hands were encircling his throat.

Something told Tinker that if he was to intervene it was now or never! He did not hesitate, despite the condition of his hands. He dared not use his automatic for fear of hitting Blake. But he could do something else, and he did it. He swung himself over the rail, and at the very moment when the Black Eagle began to switch Blake's head to one side in the killing jerk which he had mastered, Tinker jumped.

He landed clean and full between the Black Eagle's shoulders, and the force of the impact sent them both down with stunning force. Tinker rolled free and scrambled to his feet; but, quick as he was, the Black Eagle was quicker. He had been forced to loose his hold on Blake's throat, and now he threw himself in furiously to renew it.

But Blake, too, had taken that moment to recover, and as the Black Eagle came in, Blake sprang forward. He drove a terrific right to the solar plexus, and followed that with a wicked left to the point of the jaw, then with both fists he handed out all he had, getting on at last one more hard right to the "button."

A Dempsey might have weathered that last blow. Old Bob Fitzsimmons might have come back with one of his famous right hooks and weathered the storm until his spinning head had recovered. Jim Jeffries might have grunted, as used to be his wont, and even then have mustered up a grin. But the Black Eagle, husky and magnificent though he was as a fighter, and deadly though he might be with those two mighty hands of his, was not a professional heavy-weight of the first class, and, just as surely as if he had taken chloroform, did that last blow that connected with the "button" put him to sleep.

He rocked for a second, then he went down with a crash. There was a convulsive movement as some spirit within him urged him to rise; but the next moment that same spirit was swept along into the "never-never" land where nothing matters, and he lay still.

It was a beautiful knock-out.

With Tinker's assistance Blake securely bound his man while he had him helpless, then Tinker got some brandy from the tantalus in the studio, and Blake poured some of the raw spirit between the lips of his fallen foe.

It was a good ten minutes, however, before the Black Eagle came round, and at first, when he did, he seemed dazed and confused as to what had happened—until his gaze rested on the bound and gagged figure of his brother. Then intelligence came into his eyes, and he fixed his eyes on Blake.

"Your trick," he said quietly. "What are you going to do?"

"That depends entirely on you," answered Blake, as he took out his cigarette-case and lit one of the weeds. "You know, of course, what I want."

"I suppose I can guess. So you are acting for that sea-scum Bully Blood, are you?"

"Not for Bully Blood, but against you," drawled Blake. "I know just as well as you what sort of person Bully Blood is—or was. It may sound humorous, but I really intend to give Blood a chance to fulfil certain promises he has made me. By the way, my young assistant here was forced to throttle the pink macaw."

"He didn't have an easy job of it, from the look of him," shot out the Black Eagle.

"It marked him, I'll admit," said Blake, "but he owed you one for that, and I think we may say he got his own back when he jumped from the gallery a few minutes ago. But to return to our muttons. I said that you knew what I was after. I want back from you the power of attorney which Blood gave you. I also want either cash or a cheque, with which you will play no hanky-panky, for the moneys you have taken from him. Let me give you a hint of what I propose doing. I know all about why you have been carrying out a vendetta on Blood. From my point of view, you have had sufficient revenge. But I do not propose that Blood shall benefit by the money which was paid over on the wreck of his ship, the Corsair. That money—every penny of it is going back to the underwriters. And more of his money is going to those who had been marked and injured through his devilry. Blood is going to have another chance to redeem himself. I have promised him that, and I am going to keep my promise. So you know now what you have to do."

"You may promise him a chance, but he won't live to take it," snarled the Black Eagle.

"Yes, he will," rejoined Blake coldly. "I know what is the matter with him, and I have a shrewd idea just what poison it was you put in his wine that night. I can, if necessary, get an antidote from a certain man in Paris. But I shall get it from you instead. I am not particularly keen on making a police matter of this, and I realise perfectly that no case of murder could be made out against you or your brother over the killing of Bucko Breen by the pink macaw. But I have other means, and if you refuse my demands I shall use them. I may say that they include your brother. So I think you must see it is up to you."

And the Black Eagle, being a more than ordinarily intelligent man, did see.

       *   *   *   *   *

Blake kept his word to Bully Blood. And he also kept his word about other matters as well.

He gave the Black Eagle twenty-four hours to get out of England, and he held his hand with regard to the hunchback. In fact, it would have taken a very great deal to bring Blake into action against that poor atom of humanity, for none knew better than Blake that he was what others had made him, and that everything he had done had been done out of utter devotion to the Black Eagle, whom he worshipped.

And it is but fair to say that it was the consideration of his brother more than anything else that forced the Black Eagle into a complete acceptance of Blake's terms.

It was a long month before the antidote which Blake supplied to Gore's doctor did its work, for the man's frame had been terribly wasted in the illness. But at the end of that time he was able to take an active interest in his affairs, and he agreed to every condition which Blake laid down.

Every penny he was possessed of was paid into a trust fund for the benefit of those who had suffered through him, and Blake made it his business to start inquiries going to locate as many as possible.

Every penny, with the exception of ten thousand pounds, which he was allowed to keep for himself.

The hundred and fifty thousand pounds which the underwriting company had paid over was returned to them with a satisfactory explanation by Blake, and Captain Pindar was warned to get out of the country or he would find himself in trouble.

As for Bully Blood, he kept the smallest of the ships of the line he had built up, and, when he was well again, took personal command of her. He came to see Blake some months later, just before he sailed with a mixed cargo for South America, and, as he looked into the man's eyes and felt the honest, firm clasp of his hand, Blake felt a great wave of gladness pass through him, for some inner spirit of Blood's looked out at him and he knew it was the clear gleam of a regenerated soul— which was more to Sexton Blake than any other sort of triumph.

THE END.
[50000 WORDS]

Afterword

It is unusual to see the number of words cited in any story. This insertion is done because the experts at 'Fictionmags' might possibley have use for it and research work might also be facilitated. There is some rounding. From Fictionmags:

Simple Fiction Types

vi (vignette): in the context of FictionMags, "vignette" is always used to mean "short short story"

ss (short story): typically 4–20 pages (or 1,000 to 7,999 words)

nv (novelette): typically 21–50 pages (or 8,000 to 19,999 words)

na (novella/short novel): typically 51–100 pages (or 20,000 to 39,999 words)

n. (novel): typically over 100 pages (or 40,000 words or longer)

Our Magazine Corner.

Animal Assassins.

Weapons and poisons are not by any means the most effective agencies whereby the "removal" of human beings is accomplished by murderers. Animals of various kinds have been trained to the fell work, many months of patient teaching being lavished on them by the owners, who are themselves in the grip of a riot of hate against someone.

During those months the will of a dog, for example, is bent to the will of its owner, and at last there is firmly embedded in its consciousness the certainty that it will be rewarded if it carries out its master's wishes. The object of one such trainer, who was responsible for an immense sensation in the lonely country district where the tragedy ultimately occurred, was a particularly fiendish one—nothing less than the accomplishment of another's death in the most painful manner the warped and passion-drenched mind of the man could conceive.

On the outskirts of a small French village this fiend lived apart from his fellows. Not until the day dawned on the grim tragedy did anyone get an inkling of the man's occupation during the half-year that he had lived in the locality. Then it was discovered that a letter, filled with hypocritical expressions, whose tenour was a great desire to bring about a reconciliation, and re-cement a broken friendship, had brought a visitor post-haste overnight to the man's secluded house.

There a great dog had tortured him till the flame of life was extinguished. Then, in the excitement of killing, the long months of training forgotten, the dog had turned on its owner and served him the same dreadful way. From the dummy figures, with "chests" and "heads" torn to shreds, found scattered about the rounds of the house, the police were able to reconstruct the crime.

The man had taught his animal to fly at the throat of a dummy figure made up in the likeness of the man whose death he desired.

The skill shown in the training of snakes by natives of India, who allow the reptiles to retain the deadly poison-sacs behind the sharp fangs, whilst subduing them into a state in which the owner, and no one else, might handle them with impunity, is a commonplace. Time and again these trained reptiles have been employed to carry out the designs of assassins.

The training of monkeys to murder is an "art" practised almost exclusively among the murderously inclined Chinese. Only members of that strange race possess the necessary, almost limitless, patience required for the training of the tail-less monkeys selected for this purpose. For centuries it has been practised, on quite a large scale, the Chinese army purchasing numbers of these murderous animals for use in warfare.

For the latter purpose coloured flags are substituted for the dummy humans that ordinary murderers train the monkeys to attack. It may even occupy several years, but the training is persisted in until the monkey can fetch its coloured flag from a point two or three miles distant, or single out and attack the man whose dummy it has been mutilating during its long drawn-out lessons.

The Chinese army wants these beasts for purposes of shock tactics—terrorising the opposing force. The monkeys, which have been taught to pick out from several coloured flags one of particular hue, are distinguished by a dab of paint of the same colour on the back, hundreds of them will be needed by the army commander, who will, when all is in readiness, drive them into the enemy's camp, where their job is to attack the flag-bearers—with whose distinctive colours they are now familiar—and, after doing all the damage they can, to bring back the captured banners.

The loss of the flags means less even than the loss of moral consequent on the sudden invasion of starved, hunger-mad monkeys making a startling appearance out of the darkness—their bodies smeared all over with phosphorescent paint, biting and clawing creatures, whose shrieks of "Wah—wah!" rise shrill above the panic-stricken cries of the troops.

We never hear now of animals, who have been responsible for the death of humans, being brought up for trial as they were in former times. Old records tell us many strange stories of animal-trials held with tall solemnity in a court of law; how, if the animal were found guilty, sentence of death was passed on it, the sentence being duly carried out with all the pomp and ceremony ordinarily attached to the execution of a human being.

History tells us that monks of the Carthusian Order at Dijon took prominent part in the burning alive of a horse which had been tried and found guilty of kicking its master to death. Pigs that had turned on their owners and destroyed them were arrested, tried, and hanged—first being dressed in cast-off clothing, and being left suspended, after the sentence was carried out, as a warning to other animals. It was customary to erect a gallows in the market-place, and for the official hangman to carry out the duties as though he were officiating at the passing of a condemned man.

R/P

The image of an insert found in this copy of the magazine./drf

CITY OF WESTMINSTER

Copy requested herewith.

Also: Not in the Public Interest in by David Glyndwr T. WILLIAMS, Hutchinson, 1965.

with the compliments of the
Director of Leisure

The Self-made villain by David LAMPE a Lazlo SZENASI, Cassell, 1961.

Marylebone Library
Marylebone Road
London NW1 5PS
Telephone: 01-798 1206

124

www.ingramcontent.com/pod-product-compliance
Lightning Source LLC
Chambersburg PA
CBHW031837170626
46807CB00004B/1500